Differen

x

A story by Mike Tamblin

To Lynn.
Best wishes
Mike

To Emily. One day, maybe.
and
To Colin and Doreen Weir. My Kiwi "parents."
I thank you,

PublishNation

www.publishnation.co.uk

Spring 1962

The death knoll of winter had not yet started. In fact, winter looked like it was never going to go away. Autumn itself had been something of a disaster, no rain to speak of and the novelty of sunny days had long since worn off, due to the cold that the otherwise bright days carried.

No snow and even hail had failed to show up to break the monotony. Cold, pure cold, often with biting winds. No reason was forthcoming or even sought. It was just the way it was.

Even parliament had a special sitting to debate the possibility of droughts. Droughts? It wasn't even summer but dry, cold winters don't fill reservoirs.

Daffodils broke ground but failed to flower. Like as though the bud was protecting the flower within. But the would be yellow flowers were dying inside the bud, having not breathed the air that it so craved. Despite the sunshine days, the cold simply would not allow the flower to bloom.

It was a time when the Beatles were ruling the music world and "I want to hold your hand" was played almost incessantly.

Londoners were celebrating the first driverless trains on the underground and Ian Smith became Prime Minister of Rhodesia.

Here, however, a tension in the air was apparent. Before, the weather had forever been a main source of conversation, now hardly a word was spoken about it, because the story would be the same, day in and day out. Conversation itself was hard to come by, without the weather being the opening gambit. Throughout history, the weather, as a conversation had created friendships and even families, after meeting with the acknowledgement of the state of the weather. But now, people didn't even mention it. So, without this conversation, there was something of a communication breakdown. Very few smiles and a reluctance to look anyone in the eyes had replaced the optimism of the oncoming summer and the hope that it should bring. It was like a fear had gripped the nation, with sunshine

1

not necessarily bringing warmth and humanity. Many vulnerable, old and young had succumbed to the intensity of the cold by not having the funds for heating. They were bad days. Not even the rise of modern "rock and roll" music could lift the spirits of the nation, or even encourage optimism.

This was a bad time. A time that humanity had never before experienced. Maybe the time had influenced the events of the following years, we will never know.

1

Another bitterly cold day was coming to an end. At least it was Friday. A Friday that bought cheery thoughts to Julie Stapleton. Julie, the daughter of Arthur Stapleton, founder of Stapleton Haulage of Middleton, Manchester, was going to meet her boyfriend later that evening. She was anticipating "the Question". After two years of courting, James Booth had been nervous on the telephone some three hours earlier, when he'd made the plan to meet. Somewhere quiet, he insisted, somewhere nice. Julies heart fluttered at the thought.

James was from an average family but his pleasant disposition endeared him to Arthur Stapleton. The wealthy businessman. Arthur was widowed, his wife, Marian, dying of lung cancer some three years prior. But Julie, lovely Julie, his daughter, who had helped him through those bad times had now found love herself. She had made him a proud man in so many ways. This girl had gone beyond the pale to be there for her dad since the passing of his wife, making Arthur more and more hopeful that Julie would meet someone decent to settle down with and enjoy a married life, like he'd had with Marian, someone good to care for, besides himself.

Julie was pretty much running the business as well and, on this night, as so very often, was in the office long after Arthur had gone home. Or rather been sent home by his daughter.

But time was marching on and Arthur knew that Julie had an evening out with James, so at six pm, he called the office.

"You coming home soon Julie? it's 6 o'clock already and you're meeting James at 7.30, don't forget".

"I haven't forgotten Dad" she said mockingly. "Pete Thomsett is running late, should be in any moment. When he gets in I'll give him his pay then lock up. I can come in tomorrow and
    sort the paperwork".

"OK" replied Arthur. He knew she couldn't leave without paying Pete, a rough sort. Was in the army for three years and could handle himself. Good at his job too, despite his temper.

He could handle a lorry and kept it clean and tidy, as well as maintaining it himself. Could rope and sheet better than any of the other drivers and never refused a job. This time however, a different Pete Thomsett returned.

No sooner had Julie put the telephone down, she heard the unmistakeable sound of the Foden, distinct with its Gardner engine. A massive 190 horse power motor that had a low rev count, firing so rarely, you'd think it would never pull away, let alone travel the country, uphill and down dale. But with Pete at the wheel, it seemed that the lorry could go anywhere and do anything. So, as Pete negotiated the yard and parked, Julie locked the safe, after removing the pay packet. "Wow"! she thought", £11.9.6, "That's a good week for him, he'll be down at the Crown in no time".

At that, there was an almighty bang at the bottom of the wooden staircase as the bottom door was kicked open. She froze as she heard heavy footsteps hitting the risers, one, miss two, another one, miss two, miss another two. Pete Thomsett careered up the stairs, each one marked with the constant skid of rubber from previous heavy boots, the staircase walls, stained by oily hands and the handrail that really needed screwing back firmly into its rightful place, was finally wrenched from the wall. The noise of these boots landing on each step froze Julie to the spot, until BANG! The office door was kicked, almost off its hinges, shattering the small, frosted glass panel within. Then, silence. Pete stood there, panting heavily, his face bright red, his eyes bulging with sheer madness. Julie tried to scream but nothing would come. "Pppe" is all she could manage before he pounced.

4

2

Just outside Huddersfield, on the Manchester side, lies a small village named Hetthorpe. With a population of only 320, everyone pretty much knew each other. Everyone certainly knew Cynthia Morris. A pretty and plump girl of 23 with masses of ringlets in her red hair. Her blue eyes shone revealing the mischief that lay beyond them. She was vivacious and loud. Spoke her mind and didn't much care who it bothered. The truth is what it is, as far as she was concerned and if you didn't like the truth, you shouldn't create it, seemed to be her mantra.

Born to the late Minister Cecil Morris, who was minister for Hetthorpes', St Mary of the Fields and Landale Parish Church, and his wife, Elizabeth Morris. Both of whom were taken far too soon, as the result of a motor car accident. Cynthia was raised in "The Cottage by the Stream",from the age of 12 by her Aunt Margaret. A spinster, who dedicated her life to her garden and the wildlife. No-one knew how she coped financially. She had no job and apart from one or two charitable donations via the church, no other source of income. But she managed. She brought Cynthia up quite well, letting her personality grow. Both were well dressed and clean.

It was said that Cynthia was possibly brought up better with her Aunt than had she suffered the limitations of freedom, that the expectations of the church would have expected. She, in fact, flourished.

*****

On the edges of the village stood Hope Farm. A managed farm, run by the Gilbert family. George Gilbert, aged 64 and hoping for retirement, his overworked wife Marjorie aged 61 and their one and only offspring Michael. At 23, Michael was a little bit slow mentally. You could tell him nothing about farming that he didn't already know but his social skills were limited. At this point in his life, he was a virgin and, apart from family pecks, had never been kissed. He was missing not

5

having a girlfriend and, even though he didn't know what it was like to have one, knew that he needed one and that there was more to life than work. All this needed to change and soon.

The annual village dance was scheduled for this particular Friday night. Usually, it was quite an occasion but this cold start to Spring had the rural community worried. Crops were failing and livestock was suffering. The hardiest of sheep were becoming victims and the lambing season was showing all the signs of becoming a disaster. Hopefully the village dance would put some smiles on the faces of this agricultural community and help to renew confidence or even optimism. But deep down, everyone knew that this was one of those testing times, times that we all have to ride out and simply try to cope with what we have, at any given time.

In the village pub (The Anglers), the locals were gathering. Michael was there, with his farming friends, all of whom had wives and girlfriends. That didn't stop the menfolk from gathering around the bar though, to talk about farming and fretting over future sillage and hay crops. No rain to sweeten the grass and no heat to dry it. Potatoes were high on the list of topics too, until the wives decided that it was time to move over to the hall for the dance.

Even before they got to the door of the hall, the music was blaring out loud. A band, formed by local teenagers were doing their level best with music of the time, failing miserably but the volume of sound and the volume of imbibed alcohol made them sound better.

As Michael walked in, his eyes fell immediately upon Cynthia. There she was, alone in the middle of the dance floor attempting to do the Twist. They knew each other anyway but her flowing, flowery frock was showing more leg than Michael had probably ever seen before and his mouth was agape, as she gyrated without rhythm to a song she knew little of. What Michael didn't know was that Cynthia had polished off a good portion of her Aunts sherry, before leaving home. Now, at the hall, she was drinking port and lemon. Michael, however, was enthralled.

After raising his chin from the floor, he knew what he wanted and Cynthia was it. So, buoyed with porter and pushed by his pals, he plucked up the courage to go to the dance floor and join Cynthia. But, he was too late, the song ended and Cynthia dived off to the ladies toilet, with her friends in hot pursuit.

To Michael, it felt an age that she was gone and his friends noticed with great amusement what Michael was thinking, or at least, hoping for. So, they plied him with more porter, one with a brandy mixed in and convinced Michael that Cynthia was the one. And when the drinks and the cajoling started to work, again, he mustered up the courage to go and ask her for a dance.

However, he was beaten to it. Cynthia came up to him and asked HIM to dance. Luckily for Michael, the band was playing "Sealed With A Kiss". A slow one, they could steady one another rather than try to do the twist and risk both of them ending up a heap on the dance floor.

The dance went well. Afterwards, they went to a quieter part of the building to chat, after Michael had obtained another port and lemon for Cynthia. They talked about nothing really and it came as a shock to Michael when Cynthia told him that she'd had fancied him for a long time but thought that he wouldn't be interested. They talked some more until Cynthia suddenly stopped, got up and dashed outside. Michael, shocked, followed her only to be met with the sight of Cynthia paying the price for too much alcohol.

"Come on girl" he said. "I think we need to get you home".

"Are you trying to get rid of me?" she pleaded with a slur.

"No" he replied", I want to see you again".

She giggled. "Take me home then" He wrapped his arm around her and they headed off toward the cottage. She, wobbling and giggling and he, not too sure if he could take the weight, not being as sober as he'd like to have been right now. On the way to the cottage, they were passing a barn. The door was slightly open. Cynthia again giggled, she was a little better now, thanks to the cold night air. "Let's go inside" she insisted. "What??" Michael exclaimed. "Come on" she insisted. "you never done this before?" "Well" he replied but couldn't say any more as she grabbed his hand and pulled him inside. Once inside, she reached up and pulled him down and kissed him like he'd never been kissed before. She immediately noticed Michaels' inexperience and asked him, or rather told him.

"You haven't done this before, have you?"

Once again "well" was all that Michael got to say before she kissed him again, harder and more passionately.

"She was excited. "I got a virgin…..Yippee". and suddenly, with what the shocked Michael thought was one move, her frock was off, tossed over a straw bale and there she was before him. Despite the bitter cold, she stood there, still in her underwear and Michael, rigid. His eyes feasting upon her ample bosom.

"Come on Michael, come and get me". So, he did, or as best a virgin up until this point could. The whole episode lasted no more than 20 minutes and they were dressed once again and heading toward the cottage. At the gate, Michaels nerves almost went but he managed to blurt out "can I see you again?"

"You bet" she replied and, after a more, gentle kiss she went passed the gate toward the front door. Michael wasn't sure but as tipsy as he was, he was sure that Cynthia skipped her way down the path.

3

It had been almost two hours since Arthur had spoken to Julie and he was getting anxious. She was usually punctual and when she gave a time, she was true to it. After a couple of attempts of phoning the office, he considered telephoning James but though better of it, instead, he put on some warm clothes and got into his black Ford Zodiac. His dream car, there were better and more expensive cars but this was the one he wanted and Marion, bless her, indulged him.

As he gently negotiated the egress from his drive, a thought occurred that he must do something about the hedge that caused a bit of a blind spot from the right. "Better I sold up altogether" he thought. "I need something smaller, this house is too big for me and if Julie does marry James, then…Julie, yes, Julie, what on earth is she doing?" He accelerated a little harder than usual. He didn't know why, just felt that he had to get to the yard a little quicker. The road was quiet, especially for a Friday night. People were usually milling about, going from pub to pub or even the picture house. Tonight, was different. He had a bad feeling, so went a little faster still. He rounded the last corner, into Taverners Lane. Down the cobbled lane, past the Lords Taverners Inn and down to the end into the yard.

The office lights were on, so Julie must still be working, or so he thought. But the Fodens lights were still on too, the engine was still running. "Odd," Arthur heard himself saying. The lorry wasn't parked neatly with the others. Like it was abandoned. Pete was usually pedantic about these things. Always reverse parked before going to the office. His Morris Minor was still there too, so Pete must have still been around. A chill went down Arthurs spine. He walked to the downstairs door, to find it badly damaged, the latch bent by some considerable force. Panic wanted to set in but Arthur fought it back and, unlike last person to climb them, he quietly paced up the stairs sidestepping the handrail. At the top, the door of the managers' office was at a strange angle, the top hinge wrenched away from the door frame and the smashed glass crunched

9

beneath Arthurs feet. Entering further, he saw the desk, upturned. The telephone in pieces on the floor. Papers strewn menacingly all over the office, along with pens and paper clips and finally, Pete Thomsetts unopened wage packet.

"Julie?" Arthur barely whispered.

"Julie?" a little louder this time.

Silence.

"Julie!" he shouted.

A whimper came from behind the upturned desk. Hesitantly, worriedly, he peered over it and there she was. Bleeding at the mouth, her left eye swollen. The white blouse ripped apart and her black skirt was missing. A trembling Julie met Arthurs eye, frightened, hurt, damaged. Damaged in a way that no woman should be. Arthur hurriedly bent to cuddle her but she shunned him, he tried again, gently this time and she scrambled into his arms. A petrified, crying girl needing her Dad.

*****

The aftermath of this disaster rumbled on. The ambulance came and Arthur wrongly felt that there was little sympathy and it was just another job for the ambulance crew. The police turned up a whole 5 minutes after the ambulance had gone, taking Julie and Arthur to the Royal Infirmary. Two uniformed officers stumbled around the crime scene, touching, poking and even kicking potential evidence. Until a plain clothes detective arrived. He scolded the uniformed officers and made them wait by the downstairs entrance, barring anyone from entry. Meanwhile, he smoked his Park Drive cigarette, flicking ash along the way and touching articles of Julies clothing, a shoe, her skirt that had been missing, he found behind the filing cabinet. Picking it up, he poked it with a nicotine stained finger and nonchalantly dropped the skirt on the floor. A stocking was draped over the arm of the upturned swivel chair, traces of blood on the knee. Again. the article was discarded like the cigarette he'd finished some seconds before. Then there was a knock on the downstairs door.

"D S Coulson!", there was alarm in the shout.

10

"Come quick". It was one of the uniformed officers. P C Eric Stone.

"What is it Stone?"

"Sarge, I was busting, like. You know. So, I went to find the toilet, in the warehouse, just come and see".

They walked the 20 yards to the door of the warehouse and entered. Stone was shaking uncontrollably.

"What's the matter with you Stone? Pull yourself together man".

"Over there Sarge, in the corner"

And there he was. Pete Thomsett. Hanging from a rope to his neck, tied to the hook of a ceiling crane that was used for hoisting and loading heavy steel products. Not a movement, no sway but an eeriness, like the crane had realised what had happened and was paralysed by shock. Thomsetts' head was at an angle and his trousers were wet from the last function his dying body could perform. An eerie chill crept into Coulson and there was this unnatural silence. If a pin had been dropped, the echo would have reverberated around the entire warehouse.

No-one knew, or could ever work out why Thomsett would or could carry out such a heinous crime. For all that he was in temper and independence, he was a company man who was always there for the family. What drove him to it? Why? And his subsequent suicide? well, in the end, because of what he had done, no-one really cared.

His crime not only changed the life of his victim, it affected Arthur and his business too. He no longer went to the yard to run things and Julie certainly didn't. It all went downhill fast. Within 2 months, eight drivers, two mechanics and a storeman all lost their jobs, changing their lives for the worse. In fact, two of the drivers' marriages would break up as a result and children would be without their dads and the mums would have to struggle for years to come.

Yes, the attack bought a disaster to many. But worst of all, Julie. Suffering the pain and anguish of the attack, she never fully recovered. At first, James never left Julies side but then came the news, news that would prove too much for James, news that he realised was a step too far for him, he'd never cope. Julie had tried to keep it under wraps but the truth was, she was pregnant and she had to break the news to James, it was getting difficult to hide, after all. He did visit, after the news, for a while. But the visits got shorter and longer between, until they stopped altogether. Arthur took up the baton, with pride and it became he who would never leave Julies side. They both became reclusive, staying home, avoiding the prying eyes and the gossip. They didn't realise that the community was on their side, they didn't want to. Often, they would get offers of support. All were politely rebuffed. It was all too much for Julie, she felt so violated and dirty, she didn't want or realise the support and sympathy that the community had for her. Arthur was the only person she would see and, as a subsequence, was only ever going to leave the house, one more time.

4

The news was met with great excitement in Hetthorpe. It seemed that however the ethical and moral views of the time were generally adhered to and breakers of these codes were often shunned and left as objects of ridicule and gossip, this time, the news was greeted with joy. Cynthia was pregnant. Michaels very first sexual encounter had sown a seed. A seed that would change their lives forever. The village was united in their happiness for two popular members of the community, OK, they were not married, which bought a frown or two from the Church elders, especially considering Cynthias's family history but, it was deemed that this news and forthcoming event heralded a better time for the community. A sign for optimism, giving people something positive to look forward to, rather than live in the shadow of despair that the recent climate had created.

Now, the couple had a wedding to sort out and fast. They planned to marry at the registry office in Huddersfield but, because of the feeling of the villagers, the Church Deacon had agreed to let them marry in the church with full blessing. The date was set. On the day that the Americans were doing atmospheric, nuclear testing on Christmas Island, May the 12th 1962, Michael Gilbert and Cynthia Morris were to marry.

They married on one of the warmest days of the year. A further sign? Maybe not but the whole village were not going to pass this celebration up. Even the uninvited dressed up and stood outside St Mary of the Fields Church, waiting to greet the happy couple. The menfolk, possibly reluctantly, in suits and brogues that hadn't seen the light of day for many a year and with hair slicked with Brylcream, stood over their families. Some carried their prized box Brownie cameras. Wives dressed in floral dresses and fancy hats, some dabbing their tongue onto handkerchiefs to remove some offending mark from the faces of their protesting offspring. Even some teenagers, chewing gum looking cool in the fashion of the day, attended. It was a big day in Hetthorpe.

They were not to be disappointed. After what seemed to many to be an age, the ancient doors of the church opened and the strains of the Wedding march was heard, amid gasps of expectancy from the crowd. A missed note or two didn't bother them. A bunch of Michaels friends gathered outside the doors to form a guard of honour, with raised pitchforks forming an unlikely arch and women jostled for position to be the first to throw rice at the happy couple. Finally, to a huge cheer and spontaneous clapping, the new Mr and Mrs Gilbert emerged from the end of the arch of pitchforks. Michael was in his pin stripe suit, that might have come out of Al Capones wardrobe. His hair, like the rest of the men, benefiting from an overenthusiastic portion of Brylcream. But he was beaming. Cynthia? She was resplendent, in her pale, yellow lace dress, that had it not been for some strategically placed red rose patterns decency could have been questioned, though most eyes were on the telling bump. Nonetheless, complete with her white lace boater that carried a single red rose, she made a pretty bride and her bright smile and infectious giggle said it all.

The occasion was such that very few of the uninvited guests dispersed. Almost all of them followed the procession for the short walk to the village hall. Some invaded the "Anglers" so as to have some drink to salute the happy couple. At the hall, the rest strained their ears to listen to the speeches through open windows. Sandwiches, pork pies and cake was passed out to them and even the odd glass of wine. Everyone took part in this wedding. So much so, that even after Michael and Cynthia had left for a short honeymoon in Blackpool, in a borrowed Austin A55, complete with old boots and tin cans tied to the chrome bumper, the party continued. There would be sore heads the next day and kids would be tired but what the heck, it was a special occasion, enjoyed by all.

As Mr and Mrs Gilbert pulled up outside the guest house in Blackpool, it started to rain. The first for months. Gentle at first, gentle fine rain.

"Hope it's like this in the village" said Michael.

"It will be" his new wife replied. "Times are getting better".

She was right. In Hetthorpe, the rain came slightly later but it was just as welcome. Fine rain feeding the crops, sweetening the grass and putting life back into the worlds creatures, who after all had endured just the same as their human counterparts. As it got later, the rain got heaver, it poured continually, soaking the ground. In some areas, the ground was too dry to take it so quickly and let the rain run off the fields and into the lanes, causing minor floods in low lying corners. But the party continued. Grown men partied and danced in the rain, soaked to the skin and spinning their partners, wives and kids around as if to celebrate some miracle. May the 12th, in Hetthorpe was one major day.

5

The Gilberts started their life together in Elm Cottage, annexed to the farm, it was not part of the tenancy that George Gilbert was contracted to but the landlord, Sir James Roland, advised his agent to let Michael take it on at a small rental, as long as Michael made it habitable, having not had anyone live there for over 5 years. It was hard going for Michael. Long hours on the farm, then time on the cottage left little time to eat, let alone be attentive to his wife. Cynthia understood though, despite her feeling neglected at times. But she knew that Michael loved her and she adored him. So, as they entered December, the cottage was just lacking a few licks of paint. Cynthia was hoping for a Christmas baby and was happy but the child wanted to hang around for a while. The lump was huge on her, which limited her movement and she was often trying to support the small of her back with her hand, not that it did anything to help but it was something at least. On this day, she thought it would be a help to Michael if she painted the window frames in the laundry. No bending or stretching, just a little easy painting. "no problem" she thought, as she waddled her way into the room. The paint was already on the ledge, Light yellow colour, as was her choice. A screwdriver to prize the lid off and clean brush was already on the draining board. "Easy" she giggled to herself and set about her task.

It all went well. The frame was done in just over one hour and she felt great. The gentle movement had relaxed her muscles and she was moving with comfort and her confidence was growing. "Maybe I can paint the scullery door while I'm at it" she said out loud, though no-one was there to contradict her. She had to open a new tin and there was one by the door on the bottom open shelf. With screwdriver in hand, she bent to pick up the tin, when a pain struck, a severe pain in the lower abdomen. Being bent over made her dizzy and slumped into the door and down the four steps into the scullery. She was still clutching the screwdriver as she fell, as if to ease the pain but,

16

as she fell, she fell onto it, the flat end penetrating her stomach. She let out a gasp, then totally passed out.

*****

Michael, who had finished milking but not finished washing down had decided to walk the 300 yards home. He went in through back door, leaving his boots outside. He was curious that Cynthia was not in the kitchen by the open fire resting and waiting for him to come home, so he looked in the lounge.

"Cynth" he called to no reply.

"Cynth" with some alarm. "Where are you, my wife?"

He made his way out again and saw that the washroom door was open. He entered and nothing could prepare him for the sight that met him. There she was, on the floor, blood from a head wound that she suffered in the fall and another small pool of blood near her belly. Thankfully, the doctor was only just up the lane, so he ran, the fastest he'd ever run in his life, in stocking feet too and banged violently on the doctors door.

*****

Cynthia started to wake up. She looked around to see beds around her, with nurses busying themselves around the patients. She looked to the left and there was Michael, sleeping in an easy chair, his head tilted to one side with a white trail of drool out of the corner of his mouth. She felt strange. She somehow felt lighter but very sore around her stomach. A nurse noticed her stirring and came over.

"Hello Mrs Gilbert. Nice to see you awake".

This woke Michael and he snapped out of sleep and came bolt upright in his chair, a frightened look on his face.

"Cynthia, oh Cynth, what have you been up too".

"I'm not really sure" she replied, almost crying.

"Have I lost our baby"

"I'll get matron" said the nurse.

"I don't know what happened" stuttered Michael. "I came home early and found you on the laundry floor, I think that they think I did it".

"Did what?

"Stabbed you"

"Stabbed me?" tears flowing now.

"I fell, went dizzy and fell"

"You had a screwdriver stuck inside you"

"I was using it to open a tin of paint, did I kill our baby"

"No", came another voice, it was the matron. "You almost miscarried."

"Almost? Am I still pregnant"

"No" came the reply. "Nurse, if you will. please".

"A pleasure matron", but she was too intent on the conversation to do as the matron had asked.

"Your cervix didn't want to hold your baby any more" matron explained. "It wasn't strong enough".

"So, our baby, pleaded Cynthia"

"After removing the screwdriver, which thankfully didn't affect your child, we performed a procedure called a Caesarean section"......

"Our baby!" screamed Cynthia.

"Nurse", exclaimed the matron. "Would you mind?"

"My pleasure" was the reply and she semi skipped out of the ward.

"You have a baby, Mrs Gilbert. A fine and healthy baby."

The nurse quickly returned with a swathe of woollen towelling and soft sheets, in the middle was a round face, pink after his first wash and an equally pink head, aside from a covering of very fine hair that was almost blonde. Baby was sleeping soundly and suckled on its own bottom lip, unaware of the drama that surrounded its arrival. Was it dreaming? What would it dream about? Never having yet seen a life to dream about but it twitched and let out a small, comforting breath. Cynthia held out her arms, tears welling up in her eyes in sheer expectancy. Michael was a shambles, crying like the baby he had created would soon cry. He was happy, ecstatic and soon found the nerve to cuddle Cynthia as she held her new baby.

"I don't know what er, um "Cynthia uttered.

"it's a boy", said the nurse. "Born this morning at at 0132, weighing 9 pounds and 11 ounces".

"What shall we call him?" Cynthia asked Michael.

18

"Don't know", Hercules, at that size. Stuttered Michael. "You choose".

"O K, George, after your dad. You choose a second name".

"Must I?"

"Yes, he's your son, call him after you, if you like".

"No, something different, the next one can be named after me. Let me see…..Charles, I like Charles".

"Oh Michael, something different".

"Sebastian".

"No. Where's that screwdriver?"

"In your bag, the nurse thought you might like to keep it, as a reminder".

"Name please, my husband. …..Weird nurse".

"William and that's final".

"OOO". She replied. Being all tough now eh"?

"Yes, my wife, so watch it".

"Its a deal. George William it is."

"Whatever you like" replied Michael. "Dad will be chuffed though".

So, it was confirmed that at 0132pm on the 3rd of January 1963. The same day that Cliff Richard was at number one in the charts with "The next time" backed up by "Bachelor Boy". And while the Soviet spacecraft Luna attempted to reach the moon. George William Gilbert had come into the world.

*****

It was 0730 and Michael had only been gone for 20 minutes, off to spread the good news around the village and George Junior been settled in his cot beside his mum's bed, when the ward door opened. A bed was wheeled in with a heavily pregnant girl, sobbing inconsolably, followed by a white haired older gentleman, wearing a thick coat and a long woollen scarf, a worried look on his face.

"That can't be the Father" thought Cynthia, embarrassing herself at her thoughts. "Looks posh though".

No longer had that thought left her mind, when a low, almost grunting scream pierced the relative quiet of the ward.

"JULIE!!" the man shouted.

Then commotion. Doctors, nurses scurrying around in a controlled panic, tending, a doctor, issuing instructions…"no time, do it now ".

"JULIE!!" the man shouted again, before he was ushered out of the ward, all the time glancing back at the bed, hoping, worrying.

A final scream, then, the same nurse that had happily carried George Junior in a swathe of white towelling to Cynthia and Michaels' waiting arms, hastened out of the ward with another swathe. A small bundle, this time not of joy, no smile. A sense of urgency almost a tear. A further two minutes of commotion behind the curtain that had been hastily drawn around the bed, then silence. A complete contrast to 5 minutes prior. The doctor was the first to leave, head bowed, his face white, emotion drained from him. The nurses around the bed, still busy doing what they do, efficiently preparing, tidying and cleaning. The curtain often being pushed open, revealing just a glimpse of the movements they were making. Inaudible words, spoken quickly and concisely, they toiled away for a few moments longer and finally, their work was done. The curtain opened, two nurses walked on the ward side of the bed, as it was wheeled out of the ward, as if to hide something. Cynthia could see quite clearly though, that the new lady had not survived. She was tightly tucked into the bed and a sheet covered her face. At the same time as a nurse, Cynthia noticed a small pool of blood on the floor where the bed had been, the nurse scampered back and wiped it up, revealing a small tear as she did so. Cynthia knew that the lady had died but she never found out what had happened to the baby, not a clue whether it was a boy or a girl, let alone whether or not it had survived.

6

1968 and George juniors 5th year. A year that was to see the release of The Sound of music and Led Zeppelins first live performance. The Beatles were number one in the charts on Georges 5th birthday, with Hello Goodbye. Sadly, 1968 saw the deaths of Robert F Kennedy and Martin Luther King.

So far, his life had been happy. Innocence bought charm and cheek bought laughter. George Jnr could put a smile on the saddest of faces, with his natural curly hair that was never going to be controlled and a smile that could light up the darkest of places. His life was his Mobo tricycle. The streets were not safe from him, he only knew fast. Even the country lanes and the obvious dangers didn't worry him. When he wanted to go, he went. He did walk off quite a lot too, into the woods or down to the lake. In actual fact, the lake was a favourite spot for him. Mr Batrum, who lived in the village took to George in a big way. Often sending George on errands to the local shop with a note; "Please let George purchase 20 Park Drive plain" signed by Mr L Bartrum. Five years old and going to the shop and buying cigarettes. Mr Bartrum even had him buying the odd gallon of paraffin. Quite a struggle for a five year old but he never let his good old friend down. Besides, the pennies he gave for reward bought many sweets. Mr Bartrum, a keen angler, often took George with him to the lake, when he went fishing with his own son, Andrew.

On one such trip, Mr Bartrum and Andrew were patiently fishing, catching nothing, not even the odd gudgeon was biting. As for the residential pike? Nothing. George, however, was having a great day out, as usual. Running around the lake with boundless energy, possibly scaring the fish, climbing the trees and skimming pebbles across the water. At one point, he found himself on the other side of the lake. He could see Mr Bartrum and Andrew fishing and was simply going about his adventure, when he heard;

"Young man, can you help me?"

George looked back into the woods and there stood a man. Tall with white, hair. No shirt but wearing light brown trousers. He was a big man and the hairs on his chest where as white as the ones on his head. He was, however, carrying a white towel.

"I fell in the lake just now and cant reach to dry my back. Can you do it for me?"

George, innocently obliged, taking the towel and started to wipe down the mans back. It did occur to George that his back didn't appear that wet but he wiped and as wiped the man asked;

"Is my bottom wet? Hang on, I'll loosen my belt".

"GEORGE"!! came a shout from the other side of the lake. "Come here now, where I can see you".

"Sorry". Said George to the stranger. "I have to go now". And off he ran, back to Mr Bartrum, blissfully unaware of the danger he had been in.

"Where have you been?", demanded Mr Bartrum.

He explained to Mr Bartrum what had happened and Andrew was up in a flash, running around the lake and into the woods. But by now, the man was long gone.

The day ended there and then and they all went home. Nothing more was said about it, apart from George being told on no uncertain terms that he must always stay in sight.

"OK, Mr Bartrum, sorry".

And all was silent for the short journey home but George was still happy, looking into the passing fields and seeing the cattle and other animals within. Watching the white clouds against a pale blue sky. He smiled, he was happy.

7

The next few years passed innocently enough, with George being ever popular. School was no problem, quite bright, he was and with a huge circle of friends, He soon became the centre of attention. He really didn't seek attention, it just came his way. It was thought that he had his mums personality and his dads common sense. Kids, and adults alike were touched by Georges social skills. Especially Lilie Batten, so named after the flower. The same age as George, given a few weeks, she was born on March the first 1963. She lived in the village, about a half mile from the farm. Within no time, she and George became inseparable, always the first out together and the last home. They played, as kids do and talked incessantly. Mostly about nothing but always with a giggle. The woods and the fields were their playground, though Michael often found something menial for the pair of them to do around the farm. Cynthia loved seeing them around and the sight made her yearn for another child, it never happened but Lilie was a very good substitute.

However bright he was, he did have a problem with attendance. Often late for school, even making Lily late, meandering into a field, or stopping by the river to watch the fish. It was a great time, with friends aplenty, to play in the woods with, making dens, climbing trees and drinking water from the stream. His friendship with Lilie grew and they became more and more inseparable. He was gentle and kind and she liked that. Not at all like the other show off boys, that would often tug at her hair. Oddly, they never did that in front of George. Whether it was a respect for him, or a fear of him but none of them picked on, or even wanted to pick on George. So, in general, life was good for him, a time for innocent fun and a time to develop his personality, with school, a farm life and, of course, Lilie.

8

The passage of time rolled by and George, now in his eleventh year. The year that America endured the Watergate scandal and the subsequent resignation of President Nixon, with Gerald Ford becoming his successor. Times were tough once again in the UK. A recession bought about a three day working week and Northern Ireland was at the height of its troubles. People living in fear of where the next bombings would be. The rumble in the jungle saw Muhammed Ali retain his world title with a much hyped bout against George Foreman. David Essex was finally finding fame in this year and John Denver spent time at number one with "Annies Song", while the Rubettes and Alvin Stardust were well established in the UK charts. It was also the year that George and Lilie entered secondary school.

Just on the outskirts of Huddersfield, Southbank was a modern village, with a built for purpose secondary school. A high emphasis on sports, with a more than adequate Gymnasium, Tennis courts, 1 netball court 2 football fields and one rugby pitch that really saw little use. The school itself was a sprawling three story building, with a huge, well stocked library, a very able science room and the school even had gardens, where rural science was proved to be a popular lesson. Possibly because the teacher had no sense of smell, so the smokers took full advantage, sneaking into the sheds for a crafty Players number 6, or a Park Drive tipped. All bought in 5's, from the local paper shop. If lucky, they were bought in a five packet. Sometimes even a ten packet that had the other five removed would do, but often they came in a cone shaped paper bag. Very difficult to conceal, without damage to the cigarettes. Often, kids could be seen rummaging around in waste bins, searching for a fag packet.

However, a none smoker, George still enjoyed his schooling, still often late, helping dad with the milking etcetera but was still attentive. Showed a strong willingness to take on responsibilities too. This made him popular with some of the teachers but not so his mathematics teacher. Despite his personality, he was showing signs of his dads traits, where academia was not a strong point. The promise he'd shown in primary school was on the wane. He was getting slower on the uptake and needed more time to absorb information and his maths especially were proving more and more difficult for him. The maths teacher, Mr Palmer, whether understanding or not, simply didn't have the time to encourage George and possibly felt that the more time he had to take to allow George to finally let the penny drop, the less time he could devote the rest of the class, who were mostly a long way ahead of George, including Lilie. That didn't bother Lilie. Even at that age, she understood that all kids have different levels of understanding. She and George were still inseparable and still enjoyed each others' company, in school time and at home. Lilie often spending time on the farm, helping in any way she could. So George went along in his own little way, carrying the burden of not being a top scholar but was still one of the top personalities. Already, he could safely operate all the farm machinery, including the milking machines and knew about crop cycles and farrow issues, though dairy farming didn't leave a lot of time for arable farming, fields were either for grazing, hay produce or potatoes.

He was good at English and endeared himself to Mr Claire and Mr Hunter, the latter being his form teacher at that time. He showed great imagination and wit and even drama. His poetry did find a jealous side to Lilie though. She had a jealous moment, when the class was tasked by Mr Claire to write a poem, George wrote a love poem that Lilie thought was lovely.

"Did you get the kiss I sent you?
the one I blew across the sea.
Did you catch it, did you hold it?
Did you know it came from me?
Did you hold it closely, to your chest
as you walked along the shore?
Did you look to the horizon
and make a wish for more?
And tell me. When you caught it,

25

Did it make you smile?
If so, the other million sent,
would well have been worth while.

Before handing the poem to the monitor, he showed it to Lilie.

"Aww George, did you write that about me?" She asked, coyly.

"No" he replied nonchalantly.

And after a less than a minute of looking at George, in silence for what seemed an eternity, she turned away and stomped off. While Mary Smith the monitor, who's job it was to collect the poems and hand them in, read it. A small, pretty black haired girl, she stared at George with moist eyes and red face, she was immediately smitten, positively gushing at George, who didn't even notice. Being not quite 12, none of it was of any importance anyway. But he was disappointed when, at lunch break, Lily was nowhere to be seen, having sneaked out of the classroom before George. None of her friends knew where she was, even though George did have his doubts about their honesty. Even at home time, though he'd seen her in afternoon class, she was gone the second the bell rang and she didn't even come to the farm in the evening.

However, come the next day, she was at the gate, waiting for George to walk to school with her. Not a word was said about the poem, or the reasons for her avoiding George but he did notice that they'd somehow ended up holding hands all the way to school.

26

9

1976 came, bringing drought with it. The driest and hottest summer for a very long time. Potato crops were failing, as were milk yields. Hay and straw hit the highest prices they had ever hit. George Senior became more and more withdrawn, carrying the weight of the farm in drought It reminded him of the cold days of 1962/3, when the opposite weather had caused the same problems that heat was causing now. The kids loved it. Playing out every day, soaking up the sun. Those lucky enough to be in the countryside, played in the fields and the woods and could bathe in the streams and the brooks. Including George Junior. He helped where he was able but his grandfather was anxious that his grandson didn't lose out too much, on his childhood. This afforded George Junior more time to be with Lilie, which in turn, found himself getting more and more close to her. Maybe because his dad was worrying about the farm and his father, George Senior, who said little to anyone, let alone his wife, Marjorie or even Michael. Maybe, just maybe, George Junior was finding himself a little on the outside. It all felt like a lot of responsibility had fallen onto himself, who at the age of 13, felt was doing more than should have been expected around the farm, despite his Grandfathers thoughts to the contrary. But Lilie was always there, helping in any way she could. Maybe this all pushed him closer to her.

One hot day, they walked hand in hand through the woods, enjoying some time to themselves. This had been a quiet walk that they'd often done, alone. A walk that few knew of. There was no conversation, as such. Just a special togetherness. As they got to the other side of the woods, the steam, at a turn, formed something of a pool. Normal days would have seen it much deeper and steeper a drop but now, it was low and flattened out to a hard and dry mud beach. Here they lay. Lilie was shocked, when George put his arm around her shoulder and pulled her closer to him.

"Thank you Lilie". He said, with a sincerity that she'd never heard from George. He'd never been so up front. Always life and soul, kind with words but never so....so sincere.

"What for George, you OK"

"Yes, I'm fine" he replied. "it's just that we've been friends for so long that I worry that you might not realise how much I like and respect you. You've been amazing, especially over the passed few weeks of the drought. Always there, helping, carrying, caring, with never a moan and always a smile".

"George, I'm happy to help you and your family. I don't want to be anywhere else or with anyone else. What's this all about?"

"Do you remember that poem?" he asked.

"Ermmm, yes"

"I really didn't have anyone in mind when I wrote it. I just wrote it. Perhaps you put the romance into my mind.... I wish I had have said it was you I was writing about, because it would be you I would be sending millions of kisses to". I love you Lilie. Simple as that. I probably have since we were five".

Lily was speechless. Never in her life would she have expected that from George. She knew he meant it too. A hot flush embarrassed her, as George turned to her and kissed her, gently, with love and tenderness. She was a happy participant, something she'd wanted for a long time.

"I love you too George"

They kissed again. With a little more passion. Then, they laid back and spent the next hour, or more, laying there, cuddling and being blissfully happy. At a tender age, they were in love.

As they walked home, the conversation was, as normal. Life and their lives. What's to be done about the drought and chasing each other around trees and bushes. They were together. In love and very, very happy.

*****

When they reached the farm. There was a police car and an ambulance Marjorie and Cynthia were embraced in floods of

28

tears at the gate, Michael was stood in a stunned silence. Confused, white as a sheet. Then he saw his son. "George!!" He shouted. "Go to your mum, Lilie, please go home", he demanded. At that, he turned and got into the ambulance and was gone.

"I think you'd better go, Lilie ", said George, tenderly. I'll come over soon, I promise"

"What do you thinks happened?" she sobbed.

"I'll come over and tell you, when I know, remember Lilie. I love you".

As she walked away, she turned and looked to George. He was looking at his mum, his mouth wide open as he listened. He ran inside, Cynthia in hot pursuit, Marjorie, shuffling in after them.

*****

Two hours later, George was at Lilies house, inconsolable. George Senior had died, by his own hand. For reasons, only known to him. Probably, everything had all got too much and to escape his demons, he'd hanged himself from the Oak tree behind the hay barn. No letter of goodbye, or note to explain. He just decided to end his life. It was Michael who had found him. And it was

Michael who cut him down to try to resuscitate him but it was too late. Too late by a long way.

*****

Michael had returned home to his mum and Cynthia and was doing his level best to console both of them. Hiding his own feelings and trying to be strong for both, while all the time, he just wanted to break down and cry. He could have. His mum and his wife would have understood and, in fact, been there for him. Perhaps young George realised this and chose to go to Lilie. Where Lilie tried so hard for George, she couldn't give the answers to Georges seniors reasons as to why. They were both young, too young to comprehend the reasoning, or lack of it in Georges grandfathers mind. It wasn't his farm, he was a

29

manager. If the drought had made the farm go bankrupt, then it would have been the droughts fault, entirely. Why choose to leave a loving family? Lilie, poor Lilie, couldn't answer these questions. All she could do was to hold George and let him release the grief that was building up inside him. Like a dormant volcano, preparing to erupt.

It was gone 10pm, when Lilies' dad escorted George home. George had spent his final tear for that night. Mr Eric Batten made the excuse that he fancied a late stroll, to enjoy a last cigarette before bed and to cool off in the late evening breeze. He walked George to the cottage, where Michael was pacing up and down the path. With nothing more than a fleeting look Mr Batten and Michael nodded to each other in total respect. A thousand words were said in that one acknowledged nod and Mr Batten turned to go home, Michael pulled George to him and hugged him and they both walked into the cottage together. As one.

10

September came, George senior had been laid to rest at St Mary of the fields. Michael, had reluctantly taken over as farm manager. This meant that he, Cynthia and George moved into the farm house itself, with Marjorie moving into Elm cottage.

Hope farm house is a grand building, dating back to the 18th century. Five more than adequately sized bedrooms, a huge kitchen and a scullery. The lounge is immense, and the dining room could have made a small classroom. George knew his way around it, having found numerous places to hide or play as a younger boy. It took him no time to settle in. Cynthia loved it. Always dreamed of having lavish dinner parties. A quartet of musicians playing classical works in the lobby, champagne being served by an evening dressed butler, while women with black dresses, and white pinafores would wait on the guests every need. It was all a dream never to be fulfilled, however. Michael was always too busy and the social life was the odd evening over at the Anglers and the annual farmers association ball, in the village hall. All in all though, she was happy, a welcome smile, followed by an infectious giggle was always forthcoming. She adored her little family unit and nothing would change that.

It was also back to school and George had no reason to believe that this term was going to be any different to any other. He and Lilie ambled into the school, late, as usual but not by enough to cause too much concern. As he and Lily walked down the corridor, a face that George hadn't noticed in a long time approached him.

"Hello George, Remember me? Mary, Mary Smith. Haven't seen you in ages".

"Hello Mary", he replied, somewhat reluctantly and even shocked. "yes, I think I can remember you". As an image he never thought he'd acknowledged came to mind. An image of a black haired girl, that looked all red faced at him, after she'd read his poem.

31

"This is Lilie. You remember my girlfriend Lilie too, don't you?" trying to involve Lilie in a strange conversation.

"Of course I do, Hello Lilie". And that was as much of an acknowledgement Lilie would get.

"We moved away for a while but now we're back and living in Hetthorpe, just up from you." Mary digressed.

"Near Lilie"? Asked George. Desperately trying to keep Lilie in the conversation.

"Next street" came the reply. I often see you around, coming and going".

Suddenly, the call to class bell rang.

"Oh, better go" Said George. "Take care, see you around".

And off they went, thankfully, thought George, in different directions.

"What was that all about?" Asked Lilie.

"Haven't a clue" he answered. "Strange, wasn't it?".

"Yes", Lilie replied, as she held Georges hand that little bit tighter and walked that little bit closer.

*****

Over the next week or two, chance meetings between the three became more and more frequent. Always Mary seeing and approaching George and Lilie first and the conversations were always strained. Mary with her false laughter and even the odd innuendo that would leave George and Lilie embarrassed and confused in the same order. It was getting obvious that she wanted George and as little chance she had of breaking the bond between him and Lilie, made no difference. Lilie had no doubt that Mary was trying to lure George away. She was aware that George had not encouraged Mary in any way, he simply didn't have the opportunity, even had he had the desire. Lilie was far ahead of this rival, in any sense and George never had any interest, or any time for anyone else.

One afternoon, at break, Mary once again approached the couple. Before she could speak, George got the first word in.

"Mary, I'm glad that you see us as friends, and we're flattered by your attention but would you mind not seeing us quite so much. As you can see, we are a couple. We love our time together and as many friends we have hereabouts, they all let us do our thing. So please don't see us quite so often. Nothing against you but we like to keep ourselves to ourselves."

Mary was silent for what felt like forever. Her head was down and then she started to tremble. She raised her head, her face was crimson with anger And she screamed at George and Lilie.

"How dare you! What do you think you are?" she screamed. You're just a smelly farmers lad and her!!! she's a slag. You'd do so much better with me than a bitch like her".

The tirade went on and on. George took Lilie into his arms and pulled her head onto his shoulder, to let her cry freely. Himself shaking with anger an anger he couldn't let out. Then, finally, Mary stopped. Albeit briefly then, She Shouted "I hate you", turned and ran away in floods of tears. George took Lilie back into school and waited outside the girls toilets, while she calmed and got herself back together.

Suddenly, Mary reappeared.

"There he is John. he's the pig that broke my heart". Look out farm boy, my brother's going to hurt you".

"Why?" pleaded George. "I've done nothing wrong>"

"Nothing wrong? You wrote me a poem, promising me love and kisses and then led me on. I still have it here, with me" and she produced the poem. It never got handed in. "Now you push me away like a leper".

"But I didn't write it about you. Not even Lilie" It was just a poem".

Suddenly, before George could offer more defence he was hit to the side of the head with the force that felt like the weight of a medicine ball landing from a distance. No pain, just force. As he fell sideways, his head hit the now open toilet door, stunning him. Lilie had heard a commotion and was met by George being hit. She was shocked as as punch after punch rained down on Georges face and head. He tried to stand but as he stretched out his right leg, Mary' brother stamped on Georges right knee, snapping the top of the tibia. The noise sent Lilie into a screaming frenzy. But the attack continued. Kicks to the head, body, ribs breaking, ankle dislocating. The attack was relentless, until three of Georges friends barged in, taking

33

punches themselves they got the assailant to the ground, Mr Badlin, a P E teacher arrived but by now the assailant was calmed and helpless, as Mr Badlin took over and kept a good firm hold on him. Lilies girlfriends arrived and finally eased the hysterical girl and took her to the sick bay, while George lay there, unconscious, unable to be moved until the ambulance arrived. His body twisted and broken. He had been beaten beaten to within an inch of his life. Mary was nowhere to be seen.

The news reached the village in no time. Michael and Cynthia were collected from home by the school headmaster, who himself, was grief stricken. Never in his career, or in his life had he seen so much damage inflicted from one schoolboy to another. It was targeted and wholly intended. Now though, he had to be strong and steadfast in his support of Mr and Mrs Gilbert, who, bearing in mind, had only recently buried Georges grandfather. In terrible circumstances at that. Now this.

They were taken to Huddersfield Royal Infirmary. The very place where George was born and were met by the chief orthopaedic surgeon, Mr Donald Jameson. He tried to explain the extent of Georges injuries, in as simple and respectful a way he could. Among four broken ribs that had punctured a lung and the blows to the head that could be life threatening plus compound fractures to the right Fibula and tibia, it was clear that George was in a bad way. Michael and Cynthia were already at a loss of understanding, they just wanted know the facts. Is George going to die?

"It is too early to guarantee anything, Mr and Mrs Gilbert. George is very sick and is further threatened with possible infections from exposed broken bones, including his right Tibia and fibula. We still don't know the extent of further internal injuries. Kidney, Liver damage and, of course, possible brain damage. He did take quite a beating, I'm afraid.

"Enough" cried Cynthia. Please get him well again. Before fainting out of pure shock and stress.

*****

Lilie was allowed access to Georges bedside but only if accompanied by her mum, dad or Georges parents but not solo.

She was hurt by this, there was no way she was going to harm him and was heartbroken that she couldn't be close to him, alone or otherwise. They had spent so many happy hours being alone together. Why not now. They had shared stuff that neither set of parents could understand and both Lilie and George sometimes had old heads on young shoulders, such was their understanding of each other. Their life together, so far had been one of love and innocence. Not complicated by the constraints and single mindedness of adulthood. They were only at the stage of holding hands and kissing and as such, could be trusted to spend those times together, alone. Lilie was hurting. Her heart was breaking because she couldn't talk to George as she so often did. Open and honest talking. Sharing a special bond that even adults have trouble sharing.

However. After ten days of coma. A meeting of the doctors and the families, decided that Lilie could have full visiting rights, There was no set visiting time and she was given special dispensation to miss school to be with George. He wasn't going to spend his coma alone. He had his mum as a constant but she was making herself ill with lack of sleep and worry and she herself needed attention. Perhaps now that Lilie was going to be around more, Cynthia could possibly find some rest and lose some of the pressure that Lilie would happily take away from her. Michael had spent all of his spare time with his son and was himself, hurting, angry at himself for not being there as often as he wanted and needed to be but the demands of the farm made it a tough balancing act.

*****

While George was arriving at the hospital, Smith began kicking out at Georges friends. This gave him a little room to reverse kick Mr Badlins's shin, the pain causing the teacher to release his grip, just enough to give Smith, the chance to make a sprint for freedom, only to run straight into the arms of police sergeant Stone. A now burly man, free of the criticisms from the likes of Coulson, now dead from the effects of too many Park Drive. He was confident and strong. Having been in the force for 15 years by now, he'd seen and been involved in more than one altercation with desperate villains. So he had no problems with Smith. He bear hugged him, spun him and slammed him down onto the floor. While simultaneously wrenching Smiths right arm up his back. Smith let out a scream, that was totally ignored and was warned in no uncertain terms what would happen if he tried to cause any more trouble. Soon after, he was taken off to Huddersfield Police Station, after, ironically enough, being escorted to the same hospital as George to have damaged knuckles and a cut eye treated. No-one admitted as to how he received that cut, George never had a chance to get a single punch off. The cut? No-one cared but most everyone wanted to add to it. After the hospital visit, Smith was remanded in custody and, the next day, taken to a remand centre for juveniles. Maybe that was just as well, because the village was as one, in their disgust and hatred of the boy. There was no way back to Hetthorpe, or Southbank School for him, where a lynch mob mentality to "get him" was evident.

The day after, Michael came home from the hospital and slumped into the armchair. The enormity of what had happened suddenly hit him and he simply broke down in a flood of tears, rocking forward and back, sobbing like he'd never sobbed before. Why? Why? Was all he could utter.

After a couple of hours, He couldn't handle it any more. It was dusk and no-one was around, so he furtively made his way to the Smith household. Intent on retribution, he went in search of the boys father. Shaking with rage, he pushed open the gate and stumbled down the path. He was protected by a high privet hedge, so no need to creep from prying, neighbours eyes. Maybe they would have come to help, should they have known his intent. Still, he pressed on down the relatively long path, almost tripping over an old bicycle that had become mostly overgrown and had been left by the previous tenants, along with and old pram, axles and wheels missing that had probably been used to make a trolley. Michael did consider going to the front door and hammering it down but decided on stealth and crept around to the back door.

The door was originally a bold green colour, but due to lack of care, It had been left to fade, almost back to wood, in fact, a lot of the paint was peeling. More importantly, for Michael, it was open. He knocked on the frame, intentionally not too hard, hoping that no-one would hear so he could just go inside. It worked. No-one answered, so he shuffled in, sideways, as if to avoid contact with the door.

The entry took him right inside the kitchen. A sink, piled high with dirty dishes and cold dirty water. A milk bottle, half full with sour milk stood neglected. Michael didn't touch it, in fear of disturbing the contents and letting off the vile stench that usually accompanies sour milk. And in the middle of the kitchen stood a small wooden table, with only one chair for company. It had one of those blue and white checked, plastic covers, reminiscent of the 1960s. Needless to say, it was filthy, with remnants of many a meal. A cup and saucer, intact and unused. That intrigued Michael.

By now, he'd been in the kitchen for around 5 minutes, taking in the surroundings and realising how badly off, or poorly home educated the family were. He almost felt sympathetic. "No" he exclaimed to himself, remembering why he was there.

"Hello" he barked, though no answer was forthcoming. He had expected the sister to be there, or at least a parent. But no, it was all very quiet.

He, again shuffling, made his way to the lounge. The journey found himself almost wrestling with an old ironing board, another object that intrigued him and a bicycle, this time intact and obviously used. After safely negotiating these and various items of clothing, he entered a door to the right. This is where he finally met Mr Smith.

No-one knew, or certainly no-one spoke about this family. They hadn't been in the village for very long and so far, had kept themselves pretty much to themselves. It wasn't known what Mr Smith actually did for a living, or his wife, for that matter. All people knew was that they had two kids, both of whom attended Southbank School. Now, though, Michael assumed that he knew what Mr Smith was like, how he lived and what his parenting skills were. Because there he was, in front of Michael. Totally paralytic, on his side, unconscious and unresponsive. So much so, that Michael, at first, thought he was dead. Smith was wearing a pair of grey woollen socks, that had seen a poor attempt of darning. A pair of brown cord trousers, now almost smooth with wear and a green well worn woolly jumper that was worn through at the elbows. At his side, was an almost empty Bells Whiskey bottle. Whether or not he had drunk the whole of the original contents was hard to discern but it certainly smelt like it. Michael considered grabbing the bottle and hitting Smith over the head, many times with it but he didn't, he was at a loss. What Michael was most aware of, was the heat. Dangerously close to Smiths back was a two bar electric fire. Both bars were on, it wasn't even cold outside. Michael leaned over and placed his hand on Smiths back, he couldn't keep it there, it was so hot. So he pulled the plug from the socket, and rolled Smith onto his belly. Apart from a small grunt, Smith knew nothing about it.

Michael stood over Smith and shook his head in disbelief. To all intents and purposes, he'd come here to do Smith some real physical damage. Instead, he'd probably saved his life. He left via the back door and closed it behind him. No-one saw him come and no-one saw him go.

*****

Day 14 of Georges coma. Cynthia and Lilies loyalty and love, ensured that George had constant companionship. She and Cynthia took it in turns to go home to freshen up and even to eat properly. Lilie did have to attend school sometimes but nothing was ever said about her absences. Poor Michael though, he was getting by on no more than 5 hours of fitful sleep per day, working, or keeping vigil with one of the girls. There would always be two beside Georges bed. Pretty much every public visiting time, there would be a considerable number of people keeping vigil in the waiting room. All wanting to see George but the waiting room was as far as they could go but it was considered that simply being there made a difference. The whole village cared, they worried with the family and they prayed for them.

Just after lunch, on this day, Cynthia, her hair greying by the hour, fell asleep in the armchair provided. Not a very comfortable chair but buoyed up with a big pillow, she fell asleep. Fatigue finally got to her and she succumbed. She drifted to a little world of her own and perhaps dreamed of some happier time. There was the odd gentle snore but it was comforting for Lilie to know that Cynthia was actually sleeping.

Lilie took Georges hand. She held it flat to hers, so she could gently stroke the back of it. Even through the comatose state, she still felt Georges love. She'd gotten used to the odd movement of his eyelids when they sometimes twitched, as if responding to one of his own dreams. Lilie continued stroking.

"Oh George, I do hope you can hear me" she whispered, thinking that she wouldn't wake

Cynthia. "I hope and pray that you understand me and recognise my voice. I'm missing you so much. Missing talking with you as well as to you. I'm missing our walks and our time together. Your understanding of me and your patience with me".

Cynthia stirred but kept her eyes closed as she listened. Lilie was unaware.

"We still have a life George", she continued. "You will get better and then we can carry on, together"

All the time she was talking, she was head bowed, watching her own hand stroking Georges, convincing herself that every now and then, he gently squeezed hers.

"Do you remember, George, when went for that walk. Gosh, it was a hot day. We got to the pool, which was almost dry and we just lay there, on the dry mud bank, sunbathing and talking, sadly, it was the day your granddad died but we didn't know that then?" She squeezed his hand a little tighter, still looking at her hand in his.

And do you remember what you said, George? You said you loved me". A single tear escaped and landed on the back of Georges hand.

"You said that you wished that you had written that poem about me and that you would have sent those kisses to me. Well George, I'm sending mine to you. As many kisses as God will let me have, I'm giving them to you George, because I love you".

Goose pimples swam over Cynthias's body. She'd never before heard such an open outpouring of love, especially from someone so young. She held back a tear. If one had escaped, then there would have been a cascade.

Lilie gently released Georges hand and cupped her face in her own hands and quietly wept. She felt a hand gently touch the back of her shoulder. She turned around, It was Cynthia, who pursed her lips and put her index finger up to them and let out a little ssshhh, while nodding, then pointing in Georges direction. His eyes were open. A slow look left, then right, closed eyes, then open. A small tremble of his body, as if in panic or pain but soon calm again. No expression, just open eyes that appeared to be looking at the ceiling. Lilie stifled an excited scream.

"George, oh George" she uttered but to no response. She turned to Cynthia and they embraced, tightly, emotionally and relieved. Cynthia urged Lilie to find a nurse.

"Quietly, Lilie, slowly".

"Yes Cynth...Mrs Gilbert. NURSE, NURSE", She screamed, running down the corridor, tears streaming down her face.

Cynthia smiled, as she looked at George, a smile that made her realise that she wanted to do the same as Lilie. A younger Cynthia certainly would have. She also knew that Lilie had got through Georges barrier of silence and stillness. And It was then that Cynthia knew that George was coming back.

11

Georges recovery was going to be long and arduous. His initial waking from the coma was spasmodic. The first day, he simply stared at the ceiling, maybe moving his eyes left and right. Doctors ordered that the bulb be removed from the light above his bed, in fear of eye damage. The next day, his eyes stayed closed all day. The signs were good, however. Lilie and Cynthia often aware of infrequent but welcome squeezes of their hands. Whether they were deliberate or not, they didn't know but Lilie and Cynthia felt better for them.

Eventually, he did spend more time awake, looking around, the odd small smile, rather like that of a new born child, coming to terms with arrival. By now, he could actually move his head left to right. Not up and down though, which was a concern. X-rays showed nothing out of the

ordinary. Brain wise, internal swelling taking it's own time to reduce didn't help, too much pressure on the brain, hindering recovery and movement of the limbs he could have otherwise have moved himself. It was still a worrying time.

The traction on his tibia was going well and the leg would soon be in a cast. The break of the fibula was bad and being broken so close to the head, it had also dislocated from the lateral condyle. The damage done to both, meant that a permanent limp was inevitable. The lung was healing and the ribs were resealing, somehow. His nose was badly broken and so was pretty much rebuilt, more to aid breathing than for cosmetic reasons. Scarring was also inevitable and his nose was never again going to be like it was. Despite it all, he was going to recover. Time only would tell how the head injuries would affect his brain, it would be a lifetime experiment. George. Cynthia, Lilie and Michael, did what they could and exercised the limbs that could be exercised. They also all spoke to him about anything and everything, eventually a smile or two was evident.

Eventually, George made sufficient enough progress to be let out. Almost seven weeks he lay there. No fresh air to breath no sky to see or countryside to smell. Finally he was free. Albeit in a wheelchair, he was out and felt free. He had to have a bed put in the lounge, where he could benefit from interaction of the day to day life but his leg still had to be up and relatively still for a couple of weeks longer. Michael attached a rope to a ceiling beam, down to Georges bed. This meant that George could pull himself up and into the wheelchair for necessary toilet trips. He abused those trips, a little, just so he could look out of a window. Lilie did sneak him outside for short spins but his leg and body needed to be out straight for circulation, so short was short. His speech was still slurred, no-one was sure whether it was because of the pain killing drugs, or the parts of the brain that were still slightly swollen. Nonetheless, good conversation was made with all and the steady stream of visitors ensured that George was never lonely or bored. While all this went on, Lilie, Cynthia and Michael kept up the physiotherapy on his good limbs, including Georges left arm, that had also suffered a stress fracture. He was getting very strong in that one. Michaels rope had more benefits than he could have realised.

Then, the day finally came for him to have the cast removed. As he left Hope Farm, in the ambulance with Lilie, George didn't realise that there was to be a long convoy of cars leaving Hetthorpe 20 minutes after him. Michael and Cynthia obviously directly followed in their car and later, the convoy would leave. Almost the whole village were on the move. Most houses were empty. One, with a high privet hedge and a flaking green back door, which was again, open, was empty for a different reason. Gone was the bicycle from the corridor, gone was the two bar electric fire, the dirty dishes and the small kitchen table. Only the milk bottle with sour milk remained. The Smith family had left quietly one night, soon after Michaels visit. Otherwise, a happy army of villagers were on the way to Huddersfield, for a very special reason and a very special person. There was even a double decker bus, chartered for the occasion, paid for by Sir James.

The cast was removed and George felt a short but noticeable cool breeze on his skin. Red lines were there, as proof of work done and would be there forever, as if for a reminder of what had happened to him. Then, physiotherapy. George considered that the was a sadistic side to the nurse but realised that only he would benefit from her cruel to be kind attitude and effort. He struggled, at first, trying to walk in between the parallel bars. It was painful, his leg had not bared weight in weeks. He soldiered on for around half of one hour and was finally stopped by the nurse. She gave him a pamphlet of instructions and exercises for him to follow. As she gave him his crutches, she sternly advised him to DO IT, not OVERDO it.

"Don't undo all the work done and put yourself back into a painful return, I don't want to see you again", and then broke into a smile and hugged him.

George was at a loss as to why the physiotherapist, his consultant AND three or four nurses followed him down the corridor, to the exit. Until Michael opened the door and held it for George to leave first. As he did, there was a mighty roar, cheers and whistles shouts of George!, George!, filled the air. Through the sunshine and eyes full of tears, he saw over two hundred people had come to witness the deliverance of one of their own. A child of the village and a very popular one at that. Not a war hero but he might just as well have been.

12

Spring of 1977 appeared, out of nowhere. Red Rum had won the Grand National, for the third time. The Clash had there debut album release. And, It was also the time for the court case. George was to attend but it was hoped that he wouldn't have to take the stand. Smith had pleaded guilty to the offence of Grievous Bodily Harm at the magistrates court, possibly hoping for a lighter sentence. The magistrates, given the severity of the offence, the question of intent and the physical outcome, decided the case would be better heard as an adult, at the Crown Court. The date was set for Monday the 25th of April, at Huddersfield Crown Court. Soon after that decision, Smith changed his plea to NOT guilty.

A packed courtroom awaited George and he took his seat to a small ripple of applause from the gallery, accompanied by a "Good luck George" from an unidentified person, sat there within. Smith, however was greeted by loud and hateful jeers and various threats. He wasn't phased, he simply looked up to the gallery and sneered. "Go rot in hell ", someone shouted, to which turned and put up two fingers toward the gallery. Michael looked around, trying to identify the father. He couldn't. All that was in his mind, was the image of the inebriated scruffy individual that he had moved from the fire.

There was a well dressed woman, of around forty five. Jet black hair that finished just bellow the shoulder. She was probably the mother, thought Michael. Though he couldn't be sure. Since that day he'd visited the Smith house, he felt it prudent to stay well away from whoever the family might have been and as a subsequence never saw so much as a photograph of any of the Smith family, including John.

On opening, the prosecuting barrister, a Mr Alan Goodhind, a portly gentleman, highly distinguished and successful as a prosecuting barrister, addressed the jurors with a short but to the point statement.

"Ladies and gentlemen of the jury, I offer you an open and shut case of unprovoked violence, against a totally innocent victim, who's injuries were consistent with an act of grievous bodily harm....with intent. The victim simply had a girlfriend, where the assailants sister didn't have a boyfriend. It will be proved that there was no relationship between the victim and the assailants sister and the attack was no more than a thirst for blood and violence. May this case waste as little of your time as possible".

He sat down to an applause.

The defence barrister stood and was instantly met with howls of protest. "How could you defend such trash, you fool?" Was just one audible offering.

A loud bang on the oak desk from the judges gavel. Another and another, as insults were traded between Smith and the partisan gallery. Smith baiting them with sarcastic innuendo and insults.

"Silence! Silence! I will have silence in my court". Shouted Judge Allison. "One more outburst like that and I'll clear the gallery and charge you all with contempt of court. Which, I might add, carries an immediate custodial sentence. Think on that, because I shall do this, it is NOT a threat".

Another bash of the gavel, then silence.

The defence barrister, again stood and faced the jury.

Ladies and gentlemen of the Jury. How are you?" A shocked mixture of, "fine thank you" and other mumbles of indistinct offerings,

Mr Ellis, a defence barrister of many years, with mixed results. Flamboyant as he was confident. Tall and slender, with slick black hair, beneath his wig and a waxed pencil moustache.

"This is not the open and shut case, as my learned friend suggests. I offer you a trial of innocence versus arrogance, of charm and lust. I will prove that the victim is not the hero and picture of innocence that the prosecution suggest. My client, will be revealed as a boy who, as a dedicated family member, acted in protection of his sibling". Indeed, I too hope that this trial doesn't waste too much of your time but must warn you, it will not be easy.

As he sat down, the atmosphere was electric. No-one expected that opening but everyone in the court hoped that he hadn't succeeded in getting the jury onside.

The second day was a day of witnesses, that included employers of Michael and, in fact Michael himself. He came away confused and battle weary. The defence barrister had the gall to bring up the fact that George was conceived out of wedlock and that Michael and Cynthias wedding was carried out in a church in defiance of church rules and that the families had called in favours of elders and locals alike.

"They allowed you to marry in church because of the weather? "He mocked.

"It bought the village together?"

"Poppycock sir. You, your parents, their employers, your wifes Aunt, who was sister to a previous vicar, connived to try to hide the fact that your lust, yes, you the father of the victim, Your lust had got an innocent girl pregnant and you, with your family, brainwashed the village into thinking everything was all good in the world! Pah! Runs in the family, if you ask me".

That last remark was strongly objected to and the objection upheld. But, had the seed of doubt been planted. George felt uncomfortable..

Lilie was called up. She spoke volumes of good about George. About their ongoing relationship, formed at the age of five and how good a person George was and continued to be. The defence took advantage of this and turned it into something bad, furthering the evils that George had allegedly inherited from his dad, even at that tender age. It was revolting what the defence was suggesting and it caused considerable unrest in the gallery and the judge noticed.

"How far are you going with this line Mr Ellis".

"Its background your Honour, it could reveal the traits that a child can inherit", almost done your honour".

He turned to Lilie.

Lilie. Did you know that George was seeing Mary Smith behind your back"?

"He wasn't, I know he wasn't", she cried.

"And the poem he wrote to Mary"?

"What? Oh that. He didn't write it to her or about her, it was a classroom assignment. She was the monitor, given the task of collecting the poems and handing them in to Mr Claire".

"OH. So why did you leave the classroom in a hurry?"

"I'd hoped he'd written it about me but he didn't, it was just a poem".

"Did you know that Mary Smith became pregnant and that the reason you hadn't seen her in a while is because she went away to have a dangerous procedure".

"No, I didn't" but I rarely saw her out of school anyway,"

"No more questions, your honour"

If Michael had been shell shocked by the questioning, Lilie, well, she was devastated. She couldn't look at George for most of the rest of the day. She knew George hadn't been seeing Mary. Between school, work on the farm and being with Lilie all the rest of the time, it was impossible, wasn't it? As for getting Mary pregnant? No, not a chance. In all the time, alone and otherwise, he'd never laid a finger on Lilie, apart from hold her and kiss her. His innocence, like his dads, was one of his many qualities.

Lilie had to endure the rest of the day, listening to the cross examination of witness after witness. All being ripped apart by Ellis. All the good that was done by Mr Goodhind was being undone by Ellis. Once questioned, it was done. Goodhind couldn't have another go. Ellis had obviously been privy to some historic information but even then, all that mattered was now and how the jury saw it. Lilie was intelligent enough to realise this. So, at the end of the day, as the court emptied. Lilie went straight up to George and hugged him tight and told him out loud that she loved him and believed in him. Everyone from inside the courtroom saw and heard it. Everyone was moved by it, because they saw the truth, there and then. Then she kissed him. To another round of applause.

*****

The last of the following days witnesses was Mr Claire. Called mainly as a character witness, Goodind didn't question him. He felt that Mr Claire could bring about Ellis' downfall and kill off his character assassinations once and for all.

"Mr Claire, Hello sir". Said Ellis

"Hello"

"Obviously you had a lot of contact with young George here". He said, casting the smallest of glances at George. "Is he a star pupil"?

"Define star please". Was the reply.

"Is he an academic? Smart? A user?"

"I still don't know what you're asking but what I can say is, no, he's not the cleverest in school. Mathematics are a problem to him but he makes up for that in English. He is dramatic in his thoughts and considerate in what he says and does. Eloquent with his words too, oh and definitely not a user. His popularity comes from his willingness to help".

"Do you think that the eloquence of which you speak could be used to seduce and do you think he would use this eloquence for the same?"

"No, not George, he's far to good for that"

"What, in your opinion, do you think Georges uses are"?

"Well, most pupils can run rings around him mathematically and, at your age, with your experience you could do the same in a court of law. George, George is fourteen and even now could run a farm on his own. He repairs machinery and drives tractors. The mathematics of running a farm are learned from experience, sir handed down and added to by generation. How are you on a farm, Mr Ellis? a cough from Ellis and silence. "Thought not. Conjecture is a wonderful thing unless you're on the end of it".

"OK Mr Claire. What did you think of the poem"

"What poem?"

"The poem that you tasked your class to write. What did you think of Georges?"

"Didn't see it, still haven't"

"Why not"

"It wasn't handed in".

"Did that strike you as odd?"

"Yes, because George is fastidious. All his work. Maths, English. However bad or good, gets handed in. No excuses.".

"And why wasn't the poem………".

"Your conjecture suggests that Ms Smith kept it".

"No more questions your honour".

*****

Mary Smith was called and the questions from the defence were mainly based around the poem.

"Mary". Said Ellis. What made you so sure that George was interested in you?"

"He wrote that poem about me"

"Did he tell you this?"

"Yes, after Lilie left. He told her he didn't write it about her, so she went off in a huff, so he walked home with me".

"Tell me, Mary. Did anything happen, on that walk home"

"Well", she stuttered and trembled slightly and blushed. We stopped in a field, where we kissed and"

"And what Mary?"

"He did things".

"Did things, Mary? What things".

"Things I'd never done before".

"Did you let him?"

"Yes sir, he told me that he loved me".

"And after all what happened, he took you home and just... left you there?"

"He said he had to do some work on the farm".

"Did you see Him romantically again"

John Smith screamed obscenities that shocked the whole of the courtroom. Where before, you could have heard a pin drop, now chaos erupted.

"I should have finished the job and killed you farm boy". He screamed. "I will get you again, you'll see". So vitriolic, So angry.

The judge hit the gavel on the desk so hard, so many times it almost broke.

"Get that hooligan out of my court, take him down and lock him up until it's his turn!" He yelled, The ushers struggled with the handcuffed Smith. More obscenities reverberated around the court. He screamed. Spit and fought, as best he could all the way down to the cells, All the time, Mary was whimpering, "John, please don't John".

Soon, calm was restored and the questioning resumed.

"Are you alright, Mary?" Asked Ellis

The judge asked the same, adding,

49

"Are you OK to go on?"

"Yes sir, thank you sir, I'm OK".

"Mary, you were going to tell us how often you saw George after that evening",

"Apart from school, we were all in the same class, we never spoke again. He'd gone back to that Lilie". Her face twisted angrily as she scowled toward Lilie. "She stole him back".

Ellis questioned Mary for just two minutes more and ended with,

"Thank you Mary, you've been very brave".

The court adjourned for lunch and George went outside, with his parents and Lilie.

George started to cry.

"Lilie, Mum, Dad, you know that what she said was all lies, don't you? Lilie, you know that I love you, don't you? I could never do those things, never". He sobbed. Lilie, "I'm frightened, they're saying all the things that I'm not. Smith is definitely guilty, so why are they painting it all up to make it look like I deserved it? They're going to make you believe it all and you'll finish with me. But I did nothing. Nothing at all, except look for you, Lilie, when it started to get late, I ran home to help Dad".

"I know George", whispered Lilie, then held him as months of tears, that had built up out of pain and confusion, rained down his face and onto Lilies shoulder. They all hugged and cried together for a while. Emotions were running high and they all felt pretty drained. But the call was made and they had to return to the trial. Where Mr Goodhind was already at his desk, preparing to question Mary.

*****

"Mary" Asked Mr Goodhind. "You said that George had told you that he wrote the poem just for you".

"Yes sir"

"How many times did George see you before he wrote that poem"?

"Countless. We often walked home from school together".

"Really? the whole of the village and most, of the school know that George and Lilie walked home together and more

50

often than not, Lilie going to Hope farm and giving a hand. Can you say how many times you walked home from school with George and when? And did you also go straight to Hope farm?

"Mary retorted "No, I can't tell you how many times, or when and, and I went to Hope farm twice".

"Mary, I must remind you that you are under oath, so you must tell the truth. Perjury is a very serious offence. Do you understand?"

Ellis made a feeble attempt of objection, on the grounds of threatening the witness but was rebuffed.

"How many times have you been to Hope Farm?"

Mary, now trembling, stuttered. "Never, no, never".

"So really, you never walked home from school with George, did you? You never stopped in any field, never had any physical contact and you never got pregnant, did you? You simply saw the poem, that you wished was written for you, just as Lilie did. But, unlike Lilie, you concocted a story to either get George into serious trouble, or badly beaten. The latter being the case. You and Lilie are so very different".

The gallery was stirring, murmuring and a tension was brewing, and Judge Allison felt it. He tapped his gavel, with a relatively quiet,"Silence in court".

"That's not true!" Mary shouted. "I was pregnant!" Silence, stunned silence. Mary, now sniffling."but not with George and yes, I fell in love with the poem".

"If George didn't get you pregnant, then who, for heavens sake child? This boy almost died because of your lies!"

Goodhind was struggling to keep his emotions in check.

"Who was the father?"

"John". She whispered.

"Louder please, for the court".

"John! She shouted. "John Smith".

What, you're brother?"

"He's not my brother, Mum and Dad adopted him when we were both four or five". All was OK until he was eleven. Then he kept getting into trouble, fighting, stealing. He fell out with my Dad and Dad started drinking, lost his job and everything. We were both made to change schools and ended up at Southbank". Mary was calmer now. "He got interested in me last year, not long after we realised he was adopted. At first, I thought it was funny, playing at grown ups. He used to be all nice to me. One day, he found some of dads whiskey and drank some. Then", she paused, as if for breath."He forced himself on me". He hurt me but afterwards, told me it would all be OK. He even cuddled me for ages."

"But I still don't see where George comes into it?"

"Objection". Interrupted a shell shocked Ellis. "There's no need."

"Overruled. There's every need. The case is about the accused and Master Gilbert. We need to know how Smith can justify the attack."

"Mary", Said Goodhind, please continue".

"I told John and Mum and Dad that I was pregnant and I think that's why we moved to

Southbank. John was livid, at first. Had to move away from his mates and all that. But he calmed down after a while and told me that we must blame someone else. After all, people thought we were twins".

"Go on, Mary. Would you like a seat, some water?"

"No sir, thank you". She appeared relaxed now, as if a huge burden was being lifted. "When George wrote that poem, I fell in love with it and kept it. I showed it to John and he thought it would be a perfect solution to our problem. I would claim that George and me were a couple, that he'd cheated on Lilie and got me pregnant".

"So Smith attacked George for him getting you pregnant?"

"Not really sir, George politely told me the truth, that he and Lilie were a couple and he didn't want anything to do with me. I was hurt and angry. When I told John, he was furious. His plans had been messed up.

We saw George taking Lilie to the toilets to get herself sorted out, after I'd upset her. John told me to scream at George and tell him that her brother was going to hit him for breaking my heart. After promising her so much in the poem".

"I presume that's when the attack began?" Goodhind asked, though he had little to no input now. Mary was telling the story, pretty much uninterrupted. Ellis was just sitting in his chair, listening. He was almost broken. After all, he did believe their false version of events and had been certain of winning a much lighter sentence for Smith than what would have been on offer originally.

In answer to Goodhinds assumption, Mary replied.

"Yes sir, I thought he would just punch George, once or twice but he wouldn't stop. It was awful, I ran away".

Goodhind let out a long sigh.

"Thank you Mary. "No more questions from me, your honour". He said and turned away with his head bowed and felt totally drained.

*****

No more witnesses were called. It had been expected that Smith and George would have finished the week on the witness stand but Mary had saved them that. Though Smith would have wanted his time, even if just to vent his spleen and try to make liars of everyone but himself.

There was no addressing the jury with closing speeches from either barrister and Judge Allison ordered the jury to consider their verdicts on the charge of grievous bodily harm, with intent.

The Gallery emptied, with a hush of gentle murmurings. No-one could break the moment. They had all witnessed a life tragedy and witnessed a young girl become a woman at far too young an age. Maybe youthful naivety played a small part but there was no escaping the enormous part, one violent youth played in and on that naivety.

*****

It was just over one hour, when the court usher opened the doors for everyone to return to hear the verdict. As he opened the big oak doors, a thought crossed his mind that possibly, the jury had quickly reached their verdict, then went for lunch. "Over one hour", he tutted to himself and shook his head.

Smith was already in the dock, handcuffed and ankles chained. Head bowed, hiding an ashen face. Very subdued, half knowing what was going to happen. He knew there was going to be a guilty verdict but thought, on his councils advise, that he could lose the intent, substantially reducing any given sentence. Now though, after Marys's evidence, this wasn't likely.

The court room was hushed and the judge entered.

"All stand". Said in the same monotone as the previous thousand of times, prior to this occasion.

A rumble of movement. Judge Allison surveyed all that he ruled and sat. Giving everyone else the excuse to follow suit.

"Will the foreman of the jury please stand". In comparison to the clerk, the judge almost sang his words.

A spindly looking man stood, his bald patch partly covered by a wisp of hair, combed over from right to left and well dampened In an attempt to keep it in place.

"Have you reached a unanimous verdict, or a majority verdict?"

"A unanimous verdict, your honour".

"And your verdict on the charge of grievous bodily harm, with intent is?"

"Guilty".

The gallery could no longer hold back, cheers and clapping resounded around the courtroom. George and Lilie embraced and cried, while Michael and Cynthia did likewise, before embracing each other individually. It was over, their ordeal was over.

Judge Allison was a little sympathetic and himself, felt the hairs on the back of his neck stand on end, he even suffered the lump in the throat, so, he let the celebrations go on for a little longer than he felt was prudent. Then, gavel went down and all was suddenly silent.

"Will the accused please stand".

Smith was helped to his feet by two burly guards, who appreciated that as bound by chains as Smith was, nothing could be taken for granted.

"John Smith, you have been found, unanimously by a jury, to be guilty of the crime of grievous bodily harm with intent. The intent gives me little scope for leniency and given what I've witnessed from you in this very courtroom I would not necessarily be looking for any. And as for the damage done to your victim, leaving him perilously close to death. There is no doubt in my mind that you chose to cause as much injury as you possibly could. I don't believe that you might have been out of control. You planned this attack simply because your victim did the right thing, without even realising what was going on. Thus thwarting a previous plan to blacken your victims name, to protect yours.

However. I am compelled, by conscience, to consider your youth. You stand here, in an adult court, having been tried for a crime more associated with adults. Yet you are a mere fourteen years old. I feel that you do need to spend time in an adult prison, so I'm sentencing you to twelve years incarceration. You will spend the years up until your eighteenth birthday at a maximum security juvenile institution. On that day, you will be sent to an adult maximum security prison to serve out the rest of your sentence. I recommend that you serve full term. Take him down".

For the first second or two, Smith was stunned. He didn't know what to expect but twelve years years...oh no. "No", he screamed, struggling with the guards and cutting his own skin on the metal restraints. "No, no, no, no". Over and over again. All the way down the stairs and into the cells, where he could only be faintly heard.

Simultaneously, a mixed reaction from the gallery. Some cheered the verdict. Twelve years was a long time after all. But others didn't feel that it reflected how much the attack would affect George, or the ongoing rehabilitation. Plus the fact that George will spend the rest of his life with a limp. Was that taken into consideration?

George and his family were indifferent. It was all over and they all had free lives to live. Whereas Smith was going to be locked up, missing a lot of what his youth could have been and what his early adulthood might have been like, had the attack had never taken place.

Mary was never charged. Police, George, Lily and their families, felt that she had paid a price even before the attack and would possibly carry lifelong issues, as a subsequence. She was advised to seek professional help, through counselling, though not compulsory. Her father, who never attended the

55

court case, was also advised on parenting and ordered to seek help for his
alcoholism. Although Marys'smother did attend the hearing throughout, there never appeared to be any input or emotion. As the sentence was passed, she simply left, taking Mary with her.

13

Two years later, 1979 and Georges sixteenth year. His injuries meant that he missed quite a lot of school in 1978. The beginning of 1979 saw improvement but he'd missed too much education and his interest wasn't really there. So, at Easter, he left. Lilie stayed on, which was a wrench but she still called at Hope farm every day, after school and was only going to see the year out, after her exams.

The year saw one or two other changes. Georges grandmother had passed away, never having got over losing her husband in such tragic circumstances. She died peacefully and quietly, fitting to the life that she had lived. Everyone hoped that she would now find peace.

Since her passing, Elm Cottage was left unoccupied and was quickly becoming run down, due to little or no basic, ongoing maintenance and no-one showing any interest in becoming the next tenants.

Michael did mention the state of the cottage to the agent but was told, on no uncertain terms, that the cottage was not on his remit and that the farm was all that Michael had to worry about. However, Michael was a little worried. Cynthia, despite some initial doubts had become adept at bookkeeping and kept a firm grip on the purse strings, she knew virtually how every penny was earned or spent. If there was a problem, she would have known about it. The drought of 1976 did affect profits, mainly due to lower milk yields and 1977 being not much better was a time of concern but nothing to cause alarm. However, the agents attitude to Michaels concerns about Elm cottage, gave him more cause for concern. Personally, he wasn't too worried for his, or his families future because there was a more than a reasonable inheritance left to him from his mother. His parents had always been frugal with money and his father worked too hard to have holidays, or a social life, so they did manage to save considerably, with bonds and high insurances adding to already saved funds.

Three weeks after voicing his concerns, Michael and Cynthia were summoned to a meeting at the agents office in Manchester. Where they were greeted by no other than Sir James Roland. Michael hadn't seen him since before Michael became a teenager but Sir James was easily recognisable, despite the white hair and the now stooped gait. He was getting on now but still looked strong, as ever and was still as affable as Michael could remember.

The three of them entered a boardroom with a veneered ten sitting table, where the agent that Michael had spoken to sat at the head. To his right was a very well dressed lady, of around 45. She was sat crossed legged, using her knee as a bookrest. This caused her to be sitting at an angle, facing the agent and constantly appeared, or at least to Michael, to be scribbling. He was at a loss as to why she didn't use the table. Sir James placed himself at the opposite end to the agent, with Michael to his right and Cynthia to his left.

"Are we ready?" Spoke the agent. Not a man that Michael was particularly fond of.

A few uncomfortable shuffles, followed by a grunt or two, indicated that the answer was yes.

"Michael" the agent continued. "This meeting has been called by Sir James, with your interests at heart". He glanced at Cynthia and added, somewhat embarrassingly "and your family, of course".

"Let me do the talking please", Sir James interjected.

"Michael, Cynthia, the whole truth is that most of my outside interests are failing me and the droughts of 76 and 77 have cost the farm dearly. Not to mention a very expensive divorce. Beware George,"he said, wagging a mocking finger in Cynthias direction. "These women have more rights these days and now we have one as Prime Minister, it doesn't look good." and let out an embarrassing guffaw. Cynthia went to speak, "My apologies ladies". "Cynthia, I know your books are good and the farm did show a profit on both of those years but, sadly, not enough or consistent enough to help my other interests. And Michael, no other manager could have done what you have done, in such circumstances. Couple that with Georges misfortunes, well, you've been amazing".

"What are you telling us, sir?" Asked Michael.

"We're going to rent out the land Michael". Said the agent. Who didn't look too uncomfortable with the prospect.

"And Hope Farm House"? Continued Michael.

"This is the interesting part, Michael". Sir James added. "The farm house and Elm cottage are going to be sold, with a view to be turned into a specialist hotel and lodge. A place to pamper etcetera".

Cynthia started to weep. "Are we out of home and work now?"

"No dear, not yet, at least. These things all take time". Sir James attempted to reassure. "You both can be involved, in our project, if not, we'll look after you in other ways, ways that we, as a group already have agreed on".

"What would the other ways be then?"Cynthia asked.

"You explain". Sir James insisted, to the agent.

"My pleasure", was the reply.

"Michael, Sir James and all of us involved are well aware of the efforts the Gilbert family has put in to making Hope farm the successful farm that it has become, over several generations. It really is remarkable. We want to reward you and your families hard work. So yes, we will be renting two hundred and ninety four acres, in varying paddock sizes and I know that, right now, you're thinking that Sir James owns over three hundred acres. Well, the ten acre field that houses the second workshop and is south facing, Sir James wants to recognise your families efforts, by gifting this land to you and your family. If this offer is not acceptable, then, as earlier said, there would be positions for you both in the new regime, plus a financial payment as compensation. "What do you think?"

Michael and Cynthia gasped, "Can we talk about this, please, to each other". Michael spluttered.

"Certainly, old chap", laughed Sir James,"But don't take too long, will you".

"No sir, no, we won't", promised Cynthia.

The agent suggested that they arrange to meet at the farm on the following Monday morning for a further chat and a farm walk to decide how the land should be divided and, of course for values to be worked out. Michael and Cynthia could ask some questions of their own and then they could make a decision.

"Obviously, only the people in this room know of these plans. Please keep it that way, otherwise we might have to have a rethink". Said the agent.

"Yes", said Michael. "No problem".

*****

The journey home was almost tense but an excitement also filled the air. The Gilberts squabbled, then they laughed. They cried tears of what they were unsure of. Was it a win, or a loss? They finally agreed to keep quiet until they got home.

Finally home, Michael made a cup of tea and they sat at the table, just looking at their tea, letting it almost go cold.

"Have we got anything stronger?"Asked Cynthia.

"Yes but lets talk soberly, then we can have a drink to celebrate our decision. Because whatever we decide, we decide together".

They talked for over two hours. George did pop his head around the door to announce that he was off to Lilies house.

"No change there". Said Michael. They giggled.

"If we leave, where do we live", asked Michael.

"I could give notice to the tenants in the cottage". Cynthia had inherited The Cottage by the Stream from her Aunt Margaret, who died shortly after the court case and Cynthia had let it out ever since.

"We could" he replied. "Lets plan not to and see if we can use that as an insurance".

"You've made your mind up, haven't you Michael?

"Well" he mused. "Yes and no. I can't really see myself working in a hotel, for someone else and, the way I see it, If they're going to rent smaller paddocks, as well as bigger ones, not every one is going to be a farmer, so they might need a contractor to plough the fields, trim the hedges harvest their crops. I could use some of mum and dads money to buy a tractor, or rent one and buy a house. I don't know, you have a choice too".

"I know, I doubt that I'm made of hotel work either and you never tell me to do anything. You ask and if I say no, that's it. No arguments, we just do stuff and gel. And with George, we'd have a good team. Georges leg never seems to bother him, it's like he's gotten used to having a limp and does what George does. He's done well".

"True, said Michael, very true".

"Besides" Cynthia insisted. "If you and George are busy, who's going to do the paperwork". You'll never have time, or a clue". They both laughed.

"Is that a decision made" asked Michael.

"I think so. It makes sense".

"You sure?"

"Yes, "yes I am. I believe in you, my husband"

"And I believe in you, my wife.

"They sealed the deal with a kiss".

Michael found a bottle of whiskey. Not being big drinkers, there was very little alcohol in the house. He poured two large ones, then they sat on the sofa and snuggled up together.

"I've got a name for the business", she said, with her girlie giggle.

"Oh yes..What's that then".

"Gilbert and Gilbert, Contractors".

"Not Gilbert, Gilbert and Gilbert, Contractors?"

"No, too long. Just Gilbert and Gilbert".

"Who are the two Gilberts?"

"You and me". We won't tell George just yet, even though he will be a director.

They chinked glasses had a sip and went for an early night.

14

Sir James and the agent jointly considered that they had been a little hasty in agreeing to

Michael and Cynthias' requests. The couple had proved to be good hagglers and had negotiated very good terms, which include one months notice of employment termination, exclusive land maintenance contracts to any land not yet leased by Hope farm Estates and continued residence in Hope farm house, until alternative accommodation was found. A figure for a nominal rent was agreed on the condition that six months was the maximum length of tenancy. The Gilberts did offer to buy Elm Cottage but were firmly declined. Not that Michael was too worried by that, he really wanted to find somewhere that they could move into and settle, with no extra pressures of renovation. However, Michael managed to negotiate a good price for all the on site farm equipment. None of it was likely to be used by Hope Farm Estate again and Sir James had little interest in a farm sale, despite the agents protestations.

"Bah!, lots of people invading my property with no money or intention to buy anything, offering silly money for equipment. All wanting something for nothing. When all they really want it is to nose around. No, Michael is offering cash money. Must have overpaid his father, all those years, Haw Haw. Give Michael a chance and he can have the responsibility of taking it all away."

The only thing that Michael didn't buy, was the milking parlour. It's proximity was too close to the house, making it unsuitable for a potentially exclusive cottage hotel. The dairy business was to be sold off and the equipment to be sold with it.

All in all, Michael and Cynthia both felt proud of themselves for negotiating such a good deal. Hands were shaken and hugs were shared. Sir James acknowledged that it was significantly special day. It was an end to a very long and special relationship between the estate and the Gilbert families but it heralded the beginning of a new and exciting new era.

The contracts were all signed up on the fourteenth of September 1979. The date that The Knack were enjoying another week at the top of the UK music charts, with My Sharona and the Government had announced plans for the rejuvenation of the London docklands, with housing and commercial ventures. It was a good day for a lot of people and a momentous one for Michael, Cynthia and George Gilbert. Today was the day, that Gilbert and Gilbert Contractors were launched.

*****

For the first three weeks, or so. Michael and George busied themselves extending the yard space around the workshop. It cost around a half acre of land but where, at Hope farm, there was plenty of room to scatter machinery anywhere, Michael didn't have that luxury, so they had to utilise what they had. They had a barn built, butting it on to the side of the workshop, forming an L shape. plus they concreted an area of ten yards around the back of the building and squared the front of the area, making a solid working area for maintainance. The back and the sides of the building had drainage channels all the way around the workshop and in front of the barn, while the front edge of the concrete a hardcore base would encourage a water runaway. A wire fence completed a boundary. Then, they set about bringing the equipment over from Hope. It all went well and all fitted in nicely.

"A place for everything", said Michael, all satisfied with their achievement.

"Yes", said George. "As long as we can keep it this way".

Then, they started to let everyone know that they were open for business. Most of the Hope farm plots had been allocated, on long term contracts, with one or two of the smaller paddocks remaining. Michael and George kept them tidy, as per contract and, as George predicted, not all the tenants were farmers, some just wanted to dip a toe in the water to see it it was for them, while others extended their own acreage. Even the latter required Gilbert and Gilbert to help. After all, more land meant more work, leaving their current manpower and even equipment too stretched. It was early days but it was looking good for the Gilbert family businesses, as they ploughed and drilled seeds, in preparation for the coming Spring. They invested in more

machinery, including a used combine harvester, from a farm sale in Derbyshire. This, in anticipation of a good year, next year. They had to borrow for this and for the construction of another barn in which to house the harvester. The bank obviously agreed with Michaels forecast and gave him a business loan for their purchase, all secured on his property and equipment. It was the first credit that they had ever needed but were confident in their assets and indeed, their own land. And besides, the business was getting stronger and stronger. They'd even employed an experienced farm labourer, Alex Templeman. He worked under George senior at Hope farm for many years was knowledgeable on all aspects of farming and familiar with all of the equipment. The Templemans were also popular members of the village and everyone knew that it would be a good working "marriage". His wife, Norma Templeman was a tall, slender brunette that was a regular member of the church, where Alec was a reluctant follower of his wifes faith. Still, they were happy. Two young children, Amelia, born in 1972 and Steven, born in 1975, completed a good, close family.

15

Five months in and the business was going so well that they had forgotten about the their tenancy of Hope farm house nearing it's end. They hadn't looked for any other properties to buy or rent, they'd simply been too busy. A good problem to have but it sometimes gets in the way of other important issues. There had been one or two tentative viewings of the farm and Elm
cottage, from London investors and a hotel chain but no-one appeared all that interested. So Cynthia was somewhat perplexed by the agents attitude that it was imperative that the family be out on the agreed date.

"Ignore him Cynth", said Michael, giving his wife a reassuring hug. "he's an arrogant so and so. Thinks he actually owns the estate, I'm sure that Sir James won't be as pushy".

"Yes", she replied. "I know but I don't want us to put Sir James into an awkward position, so I'll start looking around tomorrow".

True to her word, by 0900 the next day, she was in Huddersfield, peering through estate agent windows, looking at renting or buying. The latter worried her a little bit, especially with the loan for the harvester hardly having the chance to breath. And while she loved the farm house, in reality, it was just too big for the three of them. "Rattling around", she thought out loud.

She came home, less confidently than she went out but with six options. Four to rent or two to buy. In honesty, she wasn't keen on any of them.

"Cynth", advised Michael. "none of them are of any use, if you have doubt. You will be spending more time in it than any of us, so your opinion is more important and more crucial".

"OK, my husband". "Love you".

"I love you too, my wife....got to go". With a peck on the cheek and a bang of the door, he was gone.

"See you later, my darling", she giggled to herself. At least later is not too late, this time of year.

Cynthia made a cup of tea and sat there, pondering as she sipped, considering all things. Her brain was churning, she was brewing, just as her tea had not too long ago been.

"Right", she shouted as she sprung from the old table chair. "Right, that's it ". She put her coat on, her wellington boots, a scarf and went out, slamming the door shut, just as Michael does every day and set off with purpose.

After just two hundred yards, her pace settled to little more than a stroll and her brain slowed, which allowed her to think a little more clearly. More thought and more consideration, iffing and butting, often talking to herself, until she suddenly found herself where she wanted to be, at the gate of "The Cottage by the Stream".

Suddenly however, she realised that the tenants were very good tenants. The cottage was kept, pretty much as Aunt Margaret would have kept it. It was clean, tidy and was still full of nostalgia and a major plus, the rent was always there on time.

"How can I even think of asking them to leave"? She was angry with herself to be thinking of it.

With that thought in mind, Cynthia turned and started to walk away.

"OOO, OOO, Cynthia". It was Violet, one of the tenants.

"Cynthia".

"Oh, hello Violet. How are you?".

"Fine thank you. Come in and have a cuppa and a chat".

"Well, I". Cynthia stuttered.

"Go on, you know you want to".

"OK". Somewhat embarrassedly she replied. "Thank you".

They entered the cottage through the front door, Cynthia, removing her boots, using the same jack that she'd used as a child, which was still painted green. She smiled to herself in that smug but cheerful way, then, she hung her coat and scarf on the hook just inside the door, before entering the lounge. She almost gasped out loud as she surveyed the room. Although it was a large lounge, the cottage charm was still in keeping with what would be expected. Cynthia had seen it on numerous occasions but for some reason it had not quite taken her aback then as it did now. The fine, white net curtains and white, with

66

red rose patterned curtains, complementing the three piece cottage suite with the same pattern. This stood on a faint green carpet. There was an oak bureaux discretely placed In one corner, behind one of the arm chairs and an oak glass cabinet stood proudly against the centre of the wall, behind the sofa. Another corner housed a low oak stool, on which stood a glazed, brown pot, home to a large Aloe plant. Cynthia was once again, in love with her aunts cottage.

"Hows Bob, Violet"?

"He's very well, thank you. I'm glad you asked because there was something I wanted to tell you".

"Oh yes", Another giggle

"No Cynthia, nothing like that and I'm not pregnant either".

They both giggled.

"Seriously though, Cynth, Bobs been offered a new job".

"Really, doing what".

"Dairy farm manager"

"No, not Hope farm?"

"Erm, no".

"Where then?" continuous giggling.

"New Zealand".

"What? But New Zealand farms are mostly about sheep, aren't they?"

"Yes but they're venturing out and reckon that dairy will take over from sheep. They have massive funding offers from China".

"Is he going to take it?"

"He has, taken it".

"Oh my word, my word. When do you go?"

"Well Bob went this morning", A little sniff.

"You're not going?"

"Yes but it was a now or never offer. I have to stay here and sort things out this end".

"Poor you"

"It's OK, it's just going to be so hard to leave here".

"How permanent a job is it?"

"Well the farm owners are paying for legal stuff like visas and are arranging everything for us. They're even paying for removal costs and flights. Free on site accommodation too.

Good, isn't it? So they seem confident, so far. Yes, it looks permanent."

"It certainly sounds like it. So, you're leaving the cottage".

"Unfortunately, yes. I was going to pop over to your place, later today but glimpsed you stood outside. That's a point. Were you coming to see us?"

"Ah, well, yes". Cynthia blurted out.

Violet poured a large glass of sherry each.

"Hmmm, rings a bell", said Cynthia, wryly.

They sat in the beautiful cottage suite, Cynthia telling stories about her life in the cottage and her purloining of copious amounts of her Aunts sherry. Even how it bought her and Michael together.

They talked and talked. Cynthia admitted as to why she was there but assured Violet that she would never have kicked them out but simply wanted to sound out Violet and Bobs thoughts.

"What are you taking?"Asked Cynthia.

"As little as possible. It's so expensive to ship it, even though we're not paying, we have to pay and claim it back. Too much hassle, plus the time it takes to get there, I might just as well sell everything and start again".

Once again, Cynthias head was spinning. She couldn't believe her luck. Once again, things were falling into place.

"Do yourself and me, a favour. Get it all valued, individually and we'll better the offer. You don't want to be robbed by unscrupulous dealers, or us. I'll even be here when valuers come, to make sure that their offers are good and fair offers. Deal?"

"Oh, deal, yes, deal", They happily shook hands and quietly counted their blessings. Though

Cynthia still had to get it passed Michael.

Later that evening, Michael arrived home from work. A little later than as of late but that's a farmers lot. You can't pin a farmer, or a contactor down, especially to meal times. Even sleep gets in their way and has to wait until the individual decides it's time to go home. He entered the kitchen to find Cynthia sat beside the fire, sipping sherry and looking quite pleased with herself. Her face was blushed but that was neither the heat, nor any embarrassment, it was the sherry. Not that she was drunk but she'd had more than she was used to, this was made obvious by the constant giggle.

"Hello, my husband", she giggled and blushed some more.

"Hello, my wife" Michael replied. Not sure whether to be amused or otherwise.

"I've been busy and I've got us sorted out. We have somewhere to live. All furnished, all tidy and all beautiful" George thought she'd slurred for most of that sentence but let her carry on. She explained all that had happened with Violet and the agreement that they had struck.

"It's a bit small, isn't it?" he mused.

"This is a bit big", she retorted. "Don't you want to live in my...our cottage? There's plenty of room. Three bedrooms, the small one can be my office, unless we add one on, where the outside loo is. You know, the one we won't use. We could even add on to the loo. I don't know. You have your little office in the workshop, We could extend that and I could work from there". It's all doable."

"What happens if me and George don't like the cottage or the furnishings?" Michael mockingly demanded.

"You're hardly ever there. The TV is just an ornament you never leave the kitchen. You eat, we chat, we go to bed". And besides all that, we don't have a stick of furniture to our name, apart from the few bits we left in Elm cottage. We have nothing to do to The Cottage by the Stream but pay for the furnishings, which are quality furnishings and move in".

"Anything else?" George asked.

"Yes!! I want to move into our cottage".

"OK" said Michael, nonchalantly.

"What?"

"OK, yes, we can move into the Cottage by the Stream".

"You! You!...Michael. I could....I love you".

Michael laughed."I knew we'd end up there sooner or later but thought it better that you decide when. Now is a good time.".

"Yes Michael, it is".

"Oh, I too have been busy negotiating", Michael teased.

"Yes, what then".

You know that last paddock, the six acre one next to our section?"

"Yes".

"I've just bought it".

"You've what??"

"You heard", Michael mocked. "Sir James came over and was quite pleased with what we'd done on our bit and with the workshop but he did have a moan about that little piece of land next to ours. No real access to it, without encroaching onto our land that little bit, was making it hard to sell, or even to rent out. He had hoped that the stable people on the other side of us would take it but they had enough on their plate to entertain the idea. So he offered it to me, for rental at first but I wasn't interested and instead, made a reasonable offer, which Sir James accepted".

"How much?" Cynthia was showing her concern about debt.

"Not enough to have to borrow but it's offset against what he pays me for work on the other untaken plots, which isn't a big loss. I'll get you to go to the bank and take out £2000. that'll cover

it, especially with your hard bargaining with Violet", he chuckled. "No, we can look after her".

"Oh, Michael. I'm so glad I met you, as drunk as I was".

"There's more, you know. Michael teased.

"Now what?"

"You remember that the new stretch of land starts wide at the top?"

"Erm, yes". She's fidgeting.

"Well, it gradually tapers down and finishes by the stream at only about fifteen feet wide".

"Go on", she said, getting anxious.

"If you climbed over the fence and walked upstream, What is the first property you arrive at?

"Don't know"

"Really?"

"Really". Bashful, sherry induced giggling.

"It's the Cottage by the Stream. How long did you live there?" He smirked.

16

Christmas 1980 came and was celebrated at the Cottage by the Stream. Lilie, her mum, Louise and Lilies' dad came over for the day, arriving at a little after 9am. Michael and George had been to work to check on the few sheep that Michael had purchased, mainly to keep the grass down in the six acres. Some had produced new lambs and those that had, had themselves and their young moved into the barn. As with all livestock, they have to be checked on, bedding straw changed and fed every day. Including Christmas. Such were the labours of the Gilberts and any other farmer. However, Michael and George had arrived home in time to greet their guests and to settle down to a fried breakfast. Dinner would be late. They had all day, after all.

While the women busied themselves in the kitchen, preparing what little Cynthia had left to prepare, the men relaxed in the lounge, drinking beer from a party seven can. Three of them, hardly seasoned drinkers, quickly found that the contents had to be drunk at a good pace, otherwise, it went flat, due to being left open for too long. So they obliged and drank the second one rather quicker than the first one. Subsequently, when the ladies retuned from the kitchen, they were met by two adults and one 17 year old, slurring and obviously a little worse for wear on little more than 4 pints each. Then, the ladies weren't about to complain, They, including Lilie had consumed more sherry than they'd realised.

"Dinnah will be sarved in half an hawa". Cynthia announced, with a mockingly posh slur, which left everyone in exaggerated, alcohol induced laughter. "Arfta tha Queens speech". She concluded.

Lilie broke away from the crowd and slipped a cassette of Christmas songs on the player. It started gently with John Lennon and Yoko Ono, singing "Merry Christmas, War Is over". That was OK, everyone joined in and it was almost pleasant. Until the next song, Slade, with "Merry Christmas Everybody" came on. Again, they all joined in, with a cats chorus of high pitched screeching. When it was over, they all collapsed into the cottage suite and laughed, tears running down each red face. None of them heard the next track because the player had been turned off and it was time for the Queens speech. Just in time and much after much ssshing from

Cynthia, the TV was turned up. There was silence, in the cottage, except for the voice of her Majesty.

In her speech, Her Majesty recognised Her mothers 80th birthday that had been celebrated in the summer and, after reflecting on her own observations of the unselfishness of doctors and nurses and people in all walks of life that choose to give their time to those in need at a time when they too could celebrate. She ended with a Tennyson poem, "Ring out wild bells".

The speech over, Cynthia roused herself to get the turkey out of the oven to breath. Lilie set the table, while Louise prepared the prawn cocktail starter, The men?.... They snored. Until Cynthia rang a rather large bell. Possibly purloined from a school or chapel. The men sprang up from their respective, seats in panic and fear, not knowing what day it was. It took them a minute or two to come to their senses and allow themselves to be led to their places at the table. Michael at the head, Cynthia opposite, George to the right of Michael, with Lily opposite. Eric was to the right of George, with Louise opposite him. Lilie changed the music and put on a cassette of Christmas Carols. The mood was now ambient, suitable for the occasion. Michael stood and went to the kitchen and returned with a bottle of champagne, plus six flute glasses, of which Cynthia knew nothing about. Michael had successfully concealed everything, not wanting to ruin the surprise.

He placed one glass beside each person and filled the glasses with quite some expertise, before returning to his own place. Then, he stood at the head of the table and very nervously, asked everyone to stand, for the Grace.

After saying Grace, everyone sat, except for Michael. All this was new to Cynthia, Grace, a speech? Michael wasn't one for speeches. Even his wedding speech was garbled, out of embarrassment. A thank you, or two, a bouquet for Aunt Margaret and the bridesmaids and some nice words for his bride. That's it. Nothing since, she sank into her chair, worried what may come out of his mouth, whether or not he was still tipsy. "Oh dear" she thought, as Michael, once again, spoke.

"Before we eat". He said. "I just want you all to know how much I value the friendship and love that you all bring to this house. My lovely wife. I thank you. My amazing son, George, I thank you. Lily, I thank you. Eric and Louise, I thank you. You have been wonderful friends to all of our family, even to my Mum and Dad. Our lives have been up and down, in recent years and the one constant has been you, the Batten family. Now, we're in our second year of business and it is going very well but for all that we have and all that we achieve, it would be nothing, without having friends like you beside us. So please stand and let me salute you all and wish you all, a very merry Christmas......MERRY CHRISTMAS.

"Merry Christmas to you too". Came the unanimous reply.

Cynthia was trying and almost failing in holding back the tears of pride that she felt right now. George was in pleasant shock, while all of the Batten family were speechless.

Finally, they all sat and ate. Talked inanely, laughed and joked, while an aura of mutual respect and happiness abounded. It was a good Christmas.

After dinner, the gifts were distributed. Everyone was overwhelmed by their gifts. They all got the usual, socks, aftershave, scents etcetera. Lilie, however was stunned. George had bought her a white gold bangle, set with three diamonds. One large one, in the middle and two smaller ones either side. She'd never seen anything so beautiful. If ever she felt loved, it was then.

By now though, Cynthia was in full flow, and so was the sherry.

"Come on then, Lets have some party games, we'll start with charades. I'll go first". She chuckled.

And she got into it thoroughly. Like the actress she never knew she wanted to be. She swayed, she swung her arms around and spun in circles until she almost fell over.

"Well, what am I ".

"Nuts, my wife". Laughed Michael.

"An Arabian Princess". Shouted Louise.

"No, sorry, though it doesn't sound a bad idea".

After much guessing and wrong answers, she agreed to let on.

"I'm a wave on the ocean".

Silence. Then laughter.

"George, your turn". She shouted.

"Aww, mum" he replied."

"Come on, coward". And everyone slow hand clapped and chanted his name until he got up.

He stood, for a second or two, before facing Lily. He struggled a little but got down onto one knee and held out his hand as if to give something to Lily. Then got up and went back to his seat.

Everyone was quiet.

"Well?" George laughingly demanded.

"It looked like you were proposing to Lilie". Said Louise

"Bang on". Said George.

"I'll do it again, with your permission, Eric".

"Erm, go on then". Was the reply, not knowing if this was for real.

So, back down on one knee, he faced Lilie.

"Lilie. I know we're young. Some might think too young but we've been together since we were five. And, in all that time. I've never wanted to be with anyone else. There is no-one that I could trust, rely on or enjoy the company of, more than you. I love you, Lilie. You are beautiful, funny and smart. And above all, you care, about everything and everyone. You are unique. You are lovely, So. Will you, Lilie Batten, please do me the honour, of becoming my wife?" Simultaneously, he produced from his pocket a small box, of which he raised the lid and offered up to Lilie. She gasped. In the box was a white gold ring, that was the replica of the bangle he'd bought her for Christmas.

She burst into tears and turned to her Mum and Dad. Chin wobbling, tears of joy streaming down her face.

"Mum, Dad", she appealed.

"It's your choice, darling", Said Louise.

"We're so proud of you". Said Eric, himself, swallowing hard and trying not to cry.

"Oh yes, George. Yes, Yes, Yes,". And jumped on top of George and hugged and kissed him, until she realised that everyone was watching, happy but watching. George then placed the ring on her finger. A perfect fit.

"How did you know the size?" She asked.

"I had just a little help", he said turning to Cynthia.

"George told me of his intentions, so I borrowed a ring that you left here one day. You'd taken it off while you were helping on the farm, so I nipped into town and got it measured. I was only gone for one hour. You probably didn't even know I'd gone anywhere.".

"We also planned the proposal". George admitted. "I got mum to start a charade and then embarrass me into doing one. No-one else knew. Just me and Mum".

"Oh George. I seem to say that a lot, don't I. I am really happy and proud to be marrying you".

Louise came over and hugged them both. "Congratulations. I knew this would happen, not today but sometime soon. My love to you both".

"Me too", said Eric as he hugged Lilie and then shook Georges hand. I'll be proud to have you as my son-in-law, George. Congratulations to both of you, Oh. After you're married, you'll be able to address each other as, My wife and My husband., just like you and Cynthia, Michael. Who started that, anyway?"

Cynthia was simply sobbing with joy. "Michael started it, immediately after we'd signed the register, "Hello my wife", he said to me, so I replied "Hello, my husband". It stuck, didn't it? Come her, you two" she giggled and sniffled at the same time. She hugged them both together and continued, "I am so, so happy. Congratulations, both of you. I am so happy, so very, very happy".

"Never noticed". Teased Michael.

"I'm very happy too", whispered Lilie , as she kissed Cynthias' cheek. "Mum two".

Finally, Michael got his turn. He pulled them both into his arms and kissed both their foreheads.

"I've always know that I've got a fantastic son. Now, I'm getting a fantastic daughter-in-law. Awesome. Congratulations".

*****

The news soon got around and new years eve at "The Anglers" and the village hall was unwittingly hijacked by the forthcoming wedding of two of it's own. The Gilbert's had once again caused a happy stir in the village.

No-one ever asked, or even considered why the Gilbert family were so popular, it was just that they were. It didn't start at Michael, or even George senior. Maybe the fact that the family were possibly part of the original inhabitants of Hetthorpe, going back countless generations.

Not mentioned in the Doomsday book, the parish believe that Hetthorpe began life as a farm or estate, shortly after the manuscript was commissioned. Possibly the farm was named Hetthorpe after the family that ran it. It all centred around the present Hope farm. The present farm house having been a large manor, that was burned down in the late 1700s and legend would tell you that a larger, grander castle stood on the same spot, until that too was raised to the ground, sometime during the civil war. The end of that war, saw the first of The Gilberts. Though that name was corrupted from a Germanic name. The family rented a small farm annexed to the new manor. A further victim to the fire that bought down the manor in it's second incarnation. It was around then that the first mention of Sir James' family came about. The Rolands rebuilt the manor but to the smaller offering that stands there today. They also built Elm cottage but that was almost half a century later. And the Battens? they could also be traced back in Hetthorpes time, going back to at least 1820. Ernest and his family being the original. He was a trader of animal feed and hides. This took him far and wide, selling his wares, often away for a week or more. The family rented a modest house, from the Rolands estate and the business was run from an adjacent stone building, originally designed for cattle but Ernest managed to persuade Lord Cecil Roland to rent it out for a nominal, cash fee.

Over the years, farming and related industries bought more and more population to the area and, indeed the present families outgrowing the family homes, meant that more and more cottages appeared. Some were tied cottages for the farm workers and others built by people from other outside industries. Once settled in Hetthorpe, few left. It had it's charm and a community grew. Even when the fifties and sixties came, bringing new council houses, to house the people from nearby factories and shops, the charm remained.

These houses were built into an estate of same shaped and uniformed dwellings. Despite the uniformity, they all looked in keeping with the countryside. The houses were built into a hillside and the bottom road curved around them, forming a tar and gravel convex moat but with little avenues going off and up into the estate that was triple decked into the hillside. Like giant theatre seats, offering their occupants the grandest of views. That's why people stayed and formed a formidable community, inspired by the spirit of the countryside.

Although, Louise Batten was an outsider, it made little or no difference to her popularity. "Outsider" was the next village, Landale. Just over one mile away. It hardly mattered, being so close made the people almost as one, in work and pleasure. Her marriage to Eric was also highly welcomed in both villages. The villages had a similar population count, which inevitably meant that pretty much everyone knew each other. Socially, if there was nothing was going on in one village, there was usually something going on in the other, especially in the early days. In fact, the interaction was such that even Erics' father had married a "Landalier" and there was a lot of other crossover marriages, of "Hetties" and "Landaliers". And Cynthias' father probably officiated over most of them, being Minister for both Parishes.

Needless to say, it came as no surprise when most of the younger villagers from Landale arrived at the Anglers, to see in the new year and to celebrate the engagement with George and Lily.

The Anglers wasn't a big pub by any imagination and Colin Firth, one of the few outsiders, a Scott was initially thrown into shock by this mass arrival but soon saw the potential for a very good night. Most of the crowd were flitting between the village hall and the pub. The hall had no alcohol licence but users could bring their own refreshments for occasions such as this. So many people bought enough from the pub to take to the hall and top up later. George and Lily were both still under age but Mr Firth turned a blind eye, after all, George only had four days to go, even though it was obvious that his pals would sneak him the odd pint. "And Lily", he thought, "her birthdays in March, what the heck". Leaving them to be adult for themselves. "If ye'r old enough to marry, ye'r old enough to drink. Go on lassie, enjoy yerself" he bellowed.

There was disco dancing in the hall, run by a young local youth, Mark Collins, who hired his equipment from a music shop in Huddersfield. He was proving to be very popular, creating something of a following for himself. Even almost finding himself with celebrity status. That was the strength of his following. He could judge an audience well and always had a good idea what they would dance to and so, would do his utmost best to play all requests asked for. Even when Cynthia wanted him to play "The Twist". Unfortunately for Michael, he found it and no sooner had the first bar been played, Cynthia was off, gyrating as she did that first night, flashing as much thigh as she did that fateful night in the sixties but this time, trying to make Michael join in. He just stood there, stout in hand and mouth open, as if in shock.

"Come on, my husband, you must remember this one".

"Only too well", he laughed.

He turned and headed for the drinks table, to watch from a safe distance.

Shortly after, the music stopped to a huge cheer. Cynthia, giggling like only Cynthia could.

"Lets hear it for Cynthia". Shouted the DJ. To which everyone obliged, loudly. Cynthia had demonstrated the twist, all on her own and in her own way. She curtseyed and giggled some more, before chasing after Michael.

"You going to walk me home tonight, my husband?" She chuckled. "Like you did all those years ago?"

"Mmmm". Said Michael, with a wink. "You never know".

"We could call in at the barn". She said, with that certain look. "You know, that barn".

"Shall we go now, my wife?" Michael was liking this idea.

"Yes please, my husband", she replied.

And they slipped out of the hall and made their way, hastily, to the barn.

Over one hour had passed and George was getting a little concerned. It was getting close to midnight and no sign of his mum and dad. He searched the hall and tried to find them in the Anglers but it was so cram packed, it was hard to discern who was who there and who wasn't.

"Anybody seen my parents?" He shouted, above the music and general cacophony of noise.

"No". Was the singular reply.

"Everyone, from the hall is going to meet in the road to see the new year in. It's not cold, so grab your drinks and we'll meet outside, if you want to join us". He announced, before racing out to find his parents.

As he got out of the car park and went to cross the road to the hall, he found them. Leaning against the wall, cuddling and giggling, of course.

"Where have you two been? I've been getting worried about you".

"We're alright". Said Cynthia, we went for a walk to get some fresh air".

"Really". Retorted, George. "Stay here, I'll get you some drinks. It looks like we're going to do the Auld Lang Syne out here".

"Who is?" Asked Michael.

"Everybody". Shouted George, in mid run.

Suddenly, he stopped and turned.

"Mum!!"

"What George, my son".

"You've got straw in your hair, my mother!"

As she and Michael hastily tried to remove the straw without messing up her hair, George ran into the hall to grab some glasses and champagne. He returned, shortly after, with Lilie and her parents, just in time to greet the new year. Everyone was there, the pub and the hall, empty. That is, except for Mark Collins, who did the countdown from the hall and Colin Firth, who did the countdown from the pub. Mark had the volume, so he played the Auld Lang Syne, which was still drowned out by the congregations varying strains and efforts. Then, while Colin set off some fireworks, the people chinked glasses, kissed and embraced, All were sincere in the wishes of a happy new year to each other, wishing prosperity and happiness. And, as George and Lilie, finally found some time together, they too embraced.

"Happy new year, My fiancée". He said.

Happy new year, my fiancé". She replied.

"Shall we start next year as Mr and Mrs?" Asked George

"What do you mean?"

"Lets get married soon, summer, perhaps".

"Oh yes please, there's nothing I would like more"

"Me too". Was the reply. "We'll make an appointment to see the minister, next week and get the ball rolling".

"I love you, George".

"I love you, Lilie".

They kissed, they cuddled and then were drawn back into the partying, which went on into the early hours. Cynthia, still with straw in her hair, wearing it with pride, danced the night away with Louise, while Michael and Eric drank champagne and looked on, moving in for the odd smooch but backing out of the more lively stuff. George and Lilie mingled, Lilie proudly showing off her engagement ring and bangle and George? He was just being proud.

17

1983 came along all too soon. George and Lilie did marry in the summer of 1981. July the 16th, in fact. A lavish affair it was too. The ceremony was held in "St Mary of the fields" church. There were a few tense moments, where Cynthias and Louises ideas clashed, Cynthia wanting the church adorned with a theme of pale yellow, with bright red roses, while Louise wanted a theme of white Lilies with Lilac freesias. So, diplomatically, Lilie took it all on herself, with Georges input. The flower theme became white Lilies and red roses, to embody love and friendship. The Lilies representing Lilie herself and her mum and the roses representing George and his mum.

Just as in 1963, when Michael and Cynthia tied their knot. George and Lilie had to walk the guard of honour on leaving the church. A corridor of twelve men, in jeans and brown smocks, held their pitchforks aloft, as the happy couple walked proudly through. At the end, hoards of people threw their confetti over the couple. Some pushing it into their clothing. It was fun, fun that everyone shared.

For the reception, Michael organised a huge marquee in the playing field, adjacent to the village hall, the hall itself was used a kitchen, cloakroom and a bar. Colin Firth got a licence to set up a temporary bar, in the hall, so he shut the pub. The whole of the village was invited to the evening celebrations, so there was no real reason to open it. Mark Collins, once again provided the music.

The speeches went well, Erics speech was straight forward, with a stumbling passage of thank you's and good wishes. He lasted for a whole minute, before embarrassment forced him to sit back down again, with a profuse sweat. But the best mans speech rallied everyone with almost endless funny anecdotes about George and his past. Suddenly though, it was Georges turn. He was quite good. Giving silver gifts to the bridesmaids Red roses with pale yellow carnations for his mum and white lilies, with lilac freesias for Louise. To end his speech, he looked at Lily and said.

81

"There are many thanks that I could offer today but first, I'd like to thank my dad for giving me the idea of how to word my speech. Remember Christmas, Dad?" Referring to Michaels pre dinner Christmas speech. "I am a blessed child. My mum and dad have always been there for me and have suffered pain because of me. They are guilty of providing a mainly happy life, where fun and hard work has merged together so well". Turning to Michael and Cynthia, he continued. "For all of it, I thank you". Turning to the guests, he continued, "For you, my family and friends, all of you have offered and given me masses of support through good and bad. All my life, you have made me feel special. If I am special, it's because of you. For that and for many other good things I thank you". Turning back to Lilie. "You Lilie. Well. You are beautiful, kind, funny, a very good friend and confidant and now.. my wife". I think I'll be thanking you over and over again for the rest of my life for all of that". After bending over and kissing her, he turned to Eric and Louise. "Eric and Louise, like everyone else, you have been there for me, as well as your own daughter. You have given me and my family so much, in support, love and friendship. Now, you have given me the ultimate gift, you have given me your daughter, your beautiful daughter. I thank you both, so very much for that. You have trusted her to me and I swear, I will never let you down". He turned back to Lilie.

"I love you, my wife"

"I love you too, my husband". She sniffled.

With a nod toward Mark, at his decks, Buddy Holly started singing, "When the girl in your arms."

*****

That was two years before and August the 1st 1983 had now arrived, bringing fear to the usually tranquil village. Wendy Marsden, six years old and the light of her parents eyes, had gone missing.

It was a balmy day, more associated with a little later in the summer but it wasn't too hot and that's why Wendy had been in the front garden, playing with her dolls and her favourite toy, Teddy. Making pretend cups of tea and even playing at being a teacher, with her dolls and Teddy being the pupils. She laughed and chatted away to her gathering of toys, that were orderly placed on the light blue and yellow bed cover, she even scolded Teddy, for being a naughty boy.

Her mum, Diane had been with Wendy for the whole of the day, barely a yard of distance had separated them, until mid afternoon, when the telephone rang. Diane got up from drinking another pretend cup of tea to go inside to answer it. She left the front door open, so she could see Wendy and she was certain that Wendy was safe. Safe, behind the privet hedge and iron gate that, it was felt, offered something of protection. Alas no.

The caller was Adrian Marsden, Wendy's dad, phoning from work at Bentons textile mill, just three miles out of Hetthorpe. He would often telephone, during his break but this time, he only called to tell Diane that he would be working late, possibly until 9pm. They chatted for a maximum of two minutes and towards the end, as usual he asked how Wendy was and was reassured by Diane that she was fine.

"Blow her a kiss for me". He asked.

"Wendy", called Diane as she peered around the door. "Daddy blew you a, Wendy? Wendy?, Wendy! WHERE ARE YOU?" She dropped the phone, letting the receiver dangle off the side of the corner table. Mothers instinct kicking in, she ran into the garden, the iron gate was open and Wendys toys, including Teddy were left on the bed sheet. "WENDY!!!" She screamed, over and over, running out into the street, hoping she was out on the pavement. "WENDY!!"". Over and over. Neighbours came out to see what was going on. Some came back to the house, to search, the phone still dangling.

"Diane, what's happening. Diane, DIANE!" To no reply.

The house, being a semi detached, offered no access to the back garden, without opening the tall, wooden side gate, which was far too high for Wendy to reach, plus an equally high garden fence, separating the next door neighbours house from Wendys, made access for a little one, impossible. And with Diane having been in the hallway on the telephone to Adrian, there was no way that Wendy could have gone back inside, without Diane seeing her. She was gone, someone had taken her.

Adrian obviously realised that something bad was going on and so, got his keys and ran out of the factory, shouting to his foreman. "Ring me". He didn't stop to clock out. He raced the three miles home, passing cars at breakneck speed only to find more hold ups around virtually every corner, making the journey time feel a lifetime. He reached Hetthorpe and turned, tyres screeching, into Harris Street and home but before he could reach his house, a policeman stood in the middle of the road, his right hand high, with a white gloved palm, demanding that the car should stop. Adrian brought the car to an abrupt halt, almost hitting the policeman and he was out of it, engine still running, he started to run towards home. The officer, however, body checked him and grabbed him tight.

"Whoa sir. Whoa. Where do you think you're going in such a hurry, who are you"?

"I'm Adrian Marsden, something's happening at my house, what is it"? He demanded.

"Are you the husband of Diane Marsden?"

"Yes, Yes, I am, what the hell is going on?"

"Come with me sir". The officer escorted Adrian through the many police cars and the gathering crowd, to home. He saw Diane, sat on the front doorstep, her head in her hands, sobbing. A policewoman beside her, her arm around Diane, offering comfort.

"Diane" Shouted Adrian.

Diane raised her head. "Adrian. Oh Adrian". She shouted, as she ran into his arms.

"What's happened?" he asked, as he pulled her head onto his chest.

"Someone has taken Wendy", she cried.

"Taken? What do you mean, taken?"

"She was on the lawn, playing, while I talked to you, I looked to blow her your kiss but she was gone, we can't find her anywhere. She hasn't even got Teddy. It's there look, on the bed cover." Diane broke down again, in floods of tears.

"What have I done? What sort of mum am I"

"Shhh, my love, shhh. Your'e a great mum. Wendy and me love. You. She'll tell you herself, when she comes home".

As he spoke, two police vans arrived. "Dog Unit" painted on the sides.

One of the officers approached.

"Mr and Mrs Marsden?" He asked, though he knew the answer. It was obvious who they were.

"Yes." They replied together.

"I'm sorry to ask but do you have any unwashed items of Wendys' clothing" Or anything else that would carry Wendys' scent".

"Yes", replied Diane. "I haven't run a wash yet, so there's bound to be plenty in the basket".

"Are there any other items in that wash, Mrs Marsden, Yours, or Mr Marsdens clothing, perhaps?"

"Yes, bits of everything really".

"Hmm, said the officer. It could confuse the dogs, having mixed scents. Anything else that might carry more of Wendys' scent".

"What about Teddy?" Asked Diane, looking at Adrian.

"Teddy?" Asked the officer.

"Teddy". Answered Adrian. "It's there, on the bed cover. She takes it everywhere. To bed, shopping with mummy, everywhere". He was struggling to hide the oncoming tears. "She will be missing it".

"OK, sir,. Do you mind if we borrow teddy for a minute or two?"

"No, choked Adrian, do whatever it takes".

He took teddy and let the dogs take in the scent, while his colleague addressed the crowd.

"Ladies and gentlemen, you obviously know what is happening here. But to reiterate, we have a missing child. Wendy Marsden. We are now going to do a foot search and if any of you would like to help, we would be more than grateful. If you have friends and family that can help, call them now. I will divide you into, within reason 50/50 strong. I and my dog, will head east with one of the 50%. My colleague and his dog, will head west, with the other 50%. If you find anything at all, like clothing, a shoe, or even a trinket. Don't touch it. Stop, hold your hand up high and shout. Don't move from that spot

85

and other officers in the search will come to you. We leave in five minutes.

The bad news travelled far, wide and fast. Louise called Lilie, who was at home doing paperwork for the business. She told Lilie all she knew and told her about the search. Louise and Eric would be going to help.

"I'll go and see George. He'll want to come and Michael, likely as not, don't know where Cynthia is though". She ended the phone call and drove over to the workshop, where Michael was working with his father.

"George, where are you?".

"In the barn". He answered, coming out, realising the alarm in her voice. "Whats up?"

"Wendy Marsden has gone missing. They think she's been kidnapped".

"Kidnapped?" He replied. It's usually rich kids that get kidnapped,,,oh no, oh no,no". He realised what the possible scenario could be.

"What George?"

"Abducted, Lilie, abducted. Oh my God".

"They've got a search party going out. Do you have time to come with me?"

"Of course I have, my wife. Please go and ring mum and your parents, I'll go and get dad".

"OK, my husband. It was mum who told me, they are already there".

The search was going to cover Hope farms land, so after contacting the police. The family waited at the workshop until the search party arrived. Hopefully, they weren't going to get that far. Wendy was going to be found safe and well at a friends house, having wandered off by herself. Not a lot different to what George used to do, at that age. But turn up, the search party did. Everyone joined in and set off in search of little Wendy Marsden.

Hope Farm house and Elm cottage, both now in a bad state, due to the failure of the agent to attract buyers for either or both, were searched but no clues were found. The search went on, in vain, well into darkness. Many reluctantly dropped out. Some because they hadn't bought torches and simply couldn't see and some had kids of their own at home. They were safe, being baby sat by family and friends that were not strong enough to take on such an arduous task as the search. But the parents out on the search were feeling a strong urge to get back to their own children. It was a gallant effort by the villagers. An effort that the police and the news people would soon, greatly acknowledged.

Sadly, that feeling of safety and that sense of community became threatened, when Henry and Celia Clarke got home from the search, to find the front door open. Henry stopped Celia from entering. Instead, he himself crept in.

"Mum". He whispered. "Mum, Peter".

In the darkness, he pushed the lounge door but it wouldn't open completely. He pushed a little harder. Still no more movement. Giving up on hope, he reached to the light switch and turned it on. he could see an outstretched arm, clad in a brown cardigan sleeve. At the wrist, the end of a white blouse cuff was exposed.

"Mum". He shouted. "Celia, phone for an ambulance".

He squeezed himself inside, to find his mother, Enid, with a huge gash to the back of her head. Blood soaked into the carpet and she was still. Her eyes were wide open, seeing nothing and she would never see anything on this earth again. There was no sign of a weapon and no sign of Peter. Henry, though in shock, was hit with a sudden sense of urgency.

"Peter". He said out loud.

He ran up the stairs and hesitated slightly, as he reached Peters bedroom. Henry opened the door, slowly and quietly. Peters red comfort light was on, as it always was, providing Peter with comfort but tonight, offering Henry, none. All it provided was enough light to show that Peters bed was empty his cover was also gone. Peter Clarke, just four years old, taken from the safety of his own home had been taken and in the process, a murder had been committed.

*****

The whole village was in a state of shock. The worst violence it had ever endured previously, was that of Georges, near death event. Everyone was asking the same questions. Was the abductor local? Does he, or she, know the families" Some people claimed to have seen a white van and some had seen a blue one. A red Lada was apparently seen to be leaving the village, at speed. All were discounted as no further descriptions were given to authenticate these sightings. No registration numbers, numbers of occupants etcetera. There was nothing at all to go on.

This came up in the conversation that the Gilbert family were having around the dining table. No food was cooked, or wanted. All were sat, round shouldered, looking down at their cups of lukewarm tea. Hurting and worrying, trying to work things out.

"Whoever it is", said Michael, "must have planned it. "Abduct Wendy, wait for a search party to go in search, then strike for the next victim while the parents were out of the way."

"Absolutely". said Lilie. "Cold and calculating but it does make sense, the only question, for me, is. Why? Why plan to take two kids one boy and one girl, of similar age, from the same village?"

"I hope the children are still, well,….alive", added Cynthia. "the poor little things must be petrified".

"Without a doubt", Said Lilie. And the poor Marsdens and the Clarkes. It doesn't bear thinking about".

George was very quiet, unusually so.

"You OK, my husband?" Lilie asked, to no answer. "George!".

He jumped. "Oh, sorry. I was just thinking, you know, families and stuff. My mum and dad, your mum and dad and me and you, Lilie. We are all from one child families. If the Marsdens and the Clarkes do lose their children, they'll have nothing". Would they want to have another child? I doubt you could ever replace a child, lost in these, or any tragic circumstances. And when would be the right time to have another child, after this?"

"Very deep for, for one so young". Said Cynthia. "Similar thoughts did cross my mind though, when we almost lost you and I really don't know the answer to that one, darling".

"You never said". Michael added.

"It was just meanderings, while sitting there, watching George, deep in his coma, his eye lids twitching and the sound of the machines, keeping him alive".

"Do you want children, George?" Asked Lilie.

"Who wouldn't want children with you, my wife? Yes, most definitely". Then he changed the subject.

"Maybe I'll walk to work tomorrow, dad. Walk along the stream a bit. You never know, something might have been missed".

"Fine, son but be careful".

"I reckon it's kids, they're after dad, not adults. I'll be OK.".

"Shall I come?" Asked Lilie.

"No thanks. Can you stay with mum and look after each other?"

"OK, my husband, good idea".

By now, it was late, so George and Lilie went home, while Michael and Cynthia went to bed. Though not much sleep would be had by either household and probably not in any other household in the village.

*****

True to his word. George was up early. He'd made breakfast for himself and Lilie and afterwards, the pair set off on the half mile walk to the Cottage by the Stream, Lilies arm hooked into Georges.

"George, I'm a bit worried about this".

"Why, I'm only going to walk along the stream, to the bottom of the six acre paddock. I don't even know why, I just feel that it's something I must do".

"Well, I have a bad feeling about it". Lilie snapped..

"Look, please stay with mum, until lunchtime and I'll take you to the pub, for a bite to eat. I'll be fine, my wife...really".

"But George" was all she could say, as they arrived at the cottage. Cynthia was already in the garden, poking and prodding at the plants, even singing to them. She looked up.

"Ah, there you are, kettles on".

"No time mum, thanks, got to get on".

"You don't have to go looking around George. Let the police do it". His mum pleaded.

"Don't you start". He retorted, before stomping off.

"What was that about?" She asked Lilie.

"I was trying to talk him out of it too but he insisted. He was a little bit angry with me, for trying to stop him".

"I have reservations about it". Said Cynthia. "Just like his dad. Get something in his head...Come on sweetie. Lets get that cuppa, then we can have a natter, while pretending to work.".

Meanwhile, George had climbed over the fence and had walked, in the middle of the shallow stream and was almost halfway to the bottom of the six acre field. He looked around at the trees that protect the other side of the stream, rising into a thicket, which tapered off back toward the stream and the six acre paddock, revealing the lay of the land, which rose for around three hundred yards, before rolling back down towards Hope Farm.

He stopped, just for a moment to look around. There was nothing to see, so he decided that Lilie and his mum were right. Nothing here for him to find and if there was, the police would find it.

As he stepped out the stream, he suddenly, heard a sharp snap, a twig being broken. He turned around quickly. No-one there. Then SNAP, another twig being broken, from his right. He spun around and was shocked to be faced with a policeman. He looked back again, to be faced with a second policeman.

"Stay where you are, sir. Don't move a muscle". Said the second officer. PC Adams, a relative newcomer to the police force, with around eighteen months of service. "Who are you and where are you off to?" he continued, getting closer to George, who was still shocked. He didn't realise that the first officer was right behind him and George back stepped one pace before, accidentally bumping into him. PC Cyril Jones was an experienced officer, 12 years in the service but had never risen above PC. While he'd always gone about his duty, in his own way, with varying results, he'd always carried bitterness at being overlooked on so many occasions. This, to him could be the icing on his cake, being one of the officers that had caught the murderer and abductor.

"Well?" Demanded PC Adams.

George told them his name and that he'd decided to have a look around, trying to help.

"Is this your land sir?"Again Adams demanded.

"Not this side, no. Our land starts over the fence, about two hundred yards that way". He pointed towards the six acre paddock. "My mum and dad live at the first cottage on the left back stream".

"So you're trespassing then?"

"Technically, I suppose so but the land owner, Sir James Roland probably wouldn't see it that way.

"So, why are you here, really?"

"I told you, a feeling, an urge to help, perhaps".

"Why would you do that, on your own, nothing you can do on your own?"

"I don't know, I just felt compelled to do it. Much against my wife and mums wishes".

"Tell you what sir, lets go down to the station and talk about this some more".

"I can't right now, I have to work. Can I pop down this evening, after work? My dads probably waiting for me already".

"Sorry, young man, it doesn't quite work like that. If you refuse, we might think that you have something to hide, so we would have to arrest you".

George became confused, started to babble and mutter, looking left and right, didn't know whether to run or just go with them. However, his decision was made and PC Jones, who had been quiet the whole time, grabbed Georges left arm from behind and snapped shut a handcuff onto his wrist and as quickly as his left wrist, his right was clapped in the other cuff. He was helpless. He started to struggle, out of pure fear but a kick, from Jones, behind his right knee, sent George stumbling to the ground. The pain was excruciating, his already damaged knee was once again under threat.

They manhandled George through the thicket and into open ground. Where, ignorant of Georges condition, dragged him over the hill and down to the grounds of Hope Farm, where their car lay in wait. Once there, they forced a now screaming George in to the back seats, before speeding off, with lights blazing and sirens wailing. Unbeknown to them, Alex Templeman, was at Hope Farm, about to set about hedge trimming on Sir James' land. He'd heard some shouting and screaming and watched, as the two policemen dragged George across the field and bundled him into their car. He didn't realise it was George, until they got close enough for him to see and not be seen.

Without hesitation, he ran over to the workshop, where Michael was working"

"Hello, Alec. You in a hurry?"

Puffing and panting, Alec related what he had seen. Michaels face paling on each word.

"Wait here, Alec."

Michael went to the telephone and phone Cynthia.

Before Cynthia could say "hello", Michael was barking out instructions.

"Cynth, you and Lilie get down to Huddersfield central police station, they've got George."

"What?" She shouted. "What for?"

"I don't know but I think they've roughed him up a bit." And ring Sir James, ask him if he can get a solicitor down there too."

Michael slammed the phone down.

"Alec". He shouted.

"Yes Mike?"

"Sorry to ask, can you come with me?"

"No need to ask boss, lets go".

On the way, Michaels mind was racing.

"Must be Huddersfield central, they've taken him to, hope so. What have they taken him for and why did they drag him around like that".

"Don't know, replied Alec. I only saw them drag poor George down the field. And the way that they forced him into the car, made my blood boil. I didn't get the policemens numbers but I got the registration of the car. That might help".

Michael went cold at the thought of his son, once again, suffering at the hands of some bully. Policemen or not, still bullies.

"After all that George has been through." He thought out loud, "Violence still visits him. He harms no-one and gives, all the time. Maybe it's time I gave some support."

"You do, Michael, all the time. You and George, you're a great team."

"Thanks Alec". But Michaels mind went back to the day that he visited the Smith household, finding a drunk, scruffy man almost cooking himself. That day, Michael was as angrier than he had ever been. Today was becoming the same.

*****

Meanwhile, the police car, driven by Adams, screeched to a halt in the police station secure parking pound. Adams and Jones dragged George out of the car by his feet, causing him to scream in pain from the knee injury. This also caused him to land face first on the tarmac. He was dragged up and into the station and hurled into a cell, where finally, they released him from the handcuffs. George wiped his face with his arm, it stung and he could see the light red blood of the gracing that the tarmac had caused, on the sleeve. His eye was swollen and bruised and, as he carefully pulled up his trouser leg, he could see that the leg was also badly bruised and swollen. Finally, he broke down and cried. The tears were in frustration not knowing why they'd treated him so badly and of anger with himself, for not heeding his wife and his mums caution.

Adams and Jones approached the custody sergeant.

"So, gentlemen. You've arrested the Hetthorpe murderer and child abductor? I heard you radio it in." Said Sergeant Stone. "Did you turn your radio off, afterwards, or something?"

"No sergeant, why?"

"Because, while you were on the way to deliver your villain to us, another victim was taken. Six year old Lucy Weaver. Similar to the Wendy Marsden case. Dad had gone to work, having kissed his daughter goodbye, her mum then left her in the lounge, to make breakfast, realised it was quiet and returned to the lounge to see if everything was OK but it wasn't, Lucy was gone. Front door wide open and not a soul to see. We did radio you but you never answered. It might interest you to know, Lucy lives three cottages downstream from the area you were patrolling.

"Maybe we didn't hear it, because Gilbert was playing up all the way."Said Jones, looking for excuses.

"Maybe, said Stone. Do you have the car keys please."

"Yes, why?"

"Lets nip out and check the radio, shall we?"

The three went out into the car pound, Adams and Jones snarling at each other, as they followed Stone to the car, who opened the drivers door and turned the ignition on.

"Look, he called, no light on the radio receiver, oh, it's turned off. We'll have to have a word about that. Now, who do we have as our guest? You said something about Gilbert. Quite a well known family of Gilberts in Hetthorpe. Is it one of them? Which one, Cynthia?" he laughed, mockingly.

"George, I think." Answered Jones.

"George. Hmm. Lets go and have a chat with him then. Lead the way Adams."

Reluctantly, Adams lead the three of them to the cells and opened the door where George, lay. Trembling, shrinking himself back into the wall.

"What the hell!" Shouted Stone. "Who did this and don't tell me he fell".

"He sort of did sergeant. He was resisting, coming out of the car, so we had to drag him out by his feet and he landed on the tarmac."

"LIAR." Shouted George. "I never resisted, Get me my father".

"Did either of these officers read you your rights. Do you know why they brought you here?"

"No, I don't even know what my rights are."

Stone turned and glared red faced at the two, not so heroic officers but before he could speak, or shout, if that was his intention, his radio cackled.

"Desk to Sergeant Stone."

"Stone".

"You need to get down here sergeant, we have a problem."

Stone looked at George. "Don't worry son, I've a feeling that your father is already here. Be calm and relax, while I sort this out".

Turning to Adams and Jones, he ordered. "You two get to the canteen and stay there, if you leave, I'll put out an arrest warrant out on you. Or you can move into the room opposite Mr Gilbert here, with the door locked. Your choice".

"I'll be back soon George, relax."

Then they were gone.

*****

Michael and Eric had arrived at the right police station and hey burst in like gangsters might have burst into a bank. The reception doors, although reinforced banging into the rubber stopper that protects the walls with such a force, you would not have known the stoppers were ever there.

"Where's my son." Michael shouted at the constable on reception. "Get my son here NOW!"

"Who do you think you are?" retorted the constable. I'll arrest you, if you keep this up."

"Arrest me! You? It'll take three like you, or more to do that. Get your boss here. I'm not dealing with a lackey, Get him here. NOW."

Cynthia and Lily arrived, in time to help Alec prevent Michael from wrecking the reception area, while the constable radioed Sergeant Stone.

"Michael, Michael, stop. What's going on?"

"I want our son and Lilies husband in front of me, so we can see what they've done to him."

Simultaneously, Sergeant Stone and Sir James arrived.

"What's going on here, George, arrested?"Demanded Sir James.

"Yes, Sir." Said Stone. "Please, everyone follow me to my office, Mr Gilbert, I will have you arrested, if you keep up this anger, OK?"

"I promise you nothing but for now, lets see."

"It's OK, sergeant, I'll look after him.", said Sir James.

A little apprehensively, sergeant Stone allowed them all to follow him to his office. Settling them in, he said, "I'll go and get George."

On the way, he popped into the canteen and told Adams and Jones to go home and stay there until called for. It was for heir own good. Though he quietly thought that Michael could have them.

At the cells, he assured George that everything was OK and that he was taking him to his family. Realising that George was struggling to get up, he asked what had happened. He also told George that he was aware of his past issues and reminded him that it was he that had pinned Smith down, after the attack.

"Would you mind if I took a look at your leg?" He asked.

"No."

They both pulled the trouser leg up as far as they could and it was plain to see that it was extremely swollen and bruised. Subsequently, walking would be a problem to George. So Stone went against protocol and sent for the family to join George in the cell, while waiting for an ambulance.

Michael was livid, as he entered the cell and saw the state that his son was in but before he had the chance to once again, explode in rage, Stone took his arm and apologised.

"Mr Gilbert, I am so very sorry this has happened. I have sent the officers involved home pending further suspension."

"Why did you send them home," Michael growled.

"Because I didn't want them and you being in the same building. The same as if it was my son, sat there." Trust me, I will get to the bottom of this, I am on your side."

The ambulance came and everyone, with the exception of Stone and Sir James went off with George. No charges were laid.

"Is Superintendent Nichols in the building." Asked Sir James.

"Yes sir."replied Stone.

"Then please tell him that I'm here and wish to speak with him. I won't be leaving and will conduct our conversation in the car park, if necessary. Do that now, old chap, will you? I'll wait in your office, if you don't mind, with a nice cup of tea, one sugar."

"I'll do that sir but the guarantee I can't make, is the quality of the tea here."

"Good old builders tea hay? That'll do fine."

After a briefing with Stone, superintendent Nichols came down to Stones office.

"James, how good to see you, come up to my office and we can discuss this matter."

96

"We'll be fine here, Claude. No secrets here, eh? Besides this won't be a discussion, this will be me, telling you what is going to happen."

"You know it doesn't work like that James. There are procedures."

"I know all about procedures, Claude, so does my barrister. You know him, Rupert Brayford. Still kicking bum, as ever, haw, haw. By the way, it's Sir James to you."

Superintendent Nichols visibly gulped hard.

"My apologies, Sir James."

Sir James explained, on no uncertain terms, what he expected. He demanded an immediate inquiry, with the threat of involving his barrister for none compliance.

"Consider it done sir. I'll be in touch."

"Good, good, see that you are. Tomorrow in the early pm will be fine. Ta Ta. Thank you for the tea, sergeant." He shouted to the door, where Stone was eavesdropping on the other side of the door. "Good man, that one. Hope he goes far."

*****

At the hospital, George was given some priority, being an emergency case and a word from Stone. His x-rays showed nothing more than heavy bruising to the knee and the outside tendon, that took a lot of the impact would be sore for a few days. Otherwise, no further damage was done to previous injuries. Pain killing anti inflammatory drugs were prescribed, along with two weeks rest. Walk was allowed with the aid of a stick. Facially, the x-rays showed a fine crack in his left cheek bone. Probably caused by hitting the wheel arch, on the way to the ground, with the grazing being caused by Adams and Jones dragging him along the tarmac. He would be pretty much be back to normal, in a couple of weeks time. Though there was concern about his mental state. Appointments were made to see a counsellor, despite Georges protestations.

It was Lilie that George was concerned about. She cared enough to tell him of her worries about going to have a look around. He didn't listen and now he was putting her through more worry. Causing her to endure more pain than she deserved. Much apologising was needed, to which Lilie would take full advantage of. Shopping, time in private and together. Stuff that can all too quickly get lost, after marriage. She easily forgave him though. She knew it was his kind heart that he had followed but on this occasion, his heart had put him in danger, from which he had luckily, once again, come through.

Right now, there were other worries. Was there going to be yet another victim of this ongoing terror? Even though Hetthorpe is a small village, the proximity of Lucy Weavers abduction was bringing it very close to Michael and Cynthias home. They felt safe inasmuch they had no young children to abduct. But there were other families with young children close by. And the worry that George had pondered, about the first two coming from a one child family, was being voiced by others, as Lucy Weaver is an only child. Now, there only six more one child families. All of whom were living in fear. Cynthia suggested that one of the families come and stay with them, at The Cottage by the Stream. Michael agreed that it was a good idea but at the same time, voiced reservations. Concerned about what length of time would be enough and would it be fair to the families that they couldn't house? If they alternated, to confuse the villain, would a pattern emerge, allowing the abductor to plan which child would be the next victim? Plus, if the abductor had a further plan, knowing which child he or she wanted to take, would anyone who protected that child, meet the same fate as Enid Clarke? It was too difficult a decision to make. Cynthias intentions, however pure and genuine, could not be implemented.

18

Five days had passed, since the last abduction and of Georges assault. After three children being abducted and one grandmother and mother having been murdered within fifteen hours of each other, the five days almost felt calm. Although those days had dragged, a sense of cautious relaxation was attempting to return. The church doors were left unlocked and people flocked, to offer their prayers and sympathy for Enid. For the Marsdens, the Clarkes and the Weavers, people were asking God to give them strength to get through this ordeal. And for the safe return of Wendy, Peter and Lucy.

There was still a large police presence, in the village. People were still being stopped and asked the same questions they'd been asked over and over again. Getting nowhere with the case, they needed to show that they were doing something.

The press were also there in force. TV camera crews, almost fighting for the best pitch, while celebrity newsreaders were constantly approaching the public, microphones in hand, to pick up any morsel of information that they could. News of Georges ordeal was kept under wraps, by the police. Even the villagers new nothing about it, except for the families involved. It was felt that it was better that the police could be left to concentrate on the investigation, rather than have to explain themselves to Hetthorpe. And the press.

Midway through that fith day, George received a telephone call.

"Mr George Gilbert?"

"Yes."

"I'm superintendent Nichols, of Huddersfield central police station. I've been liaising with my superiors, Sir James Roland and the two officers involved in your case and was wondering. Is it all possible that you and your family could come down for a meeting? Sir James is already here, so there is no need to contact him.

"What, today?" Asked George. "A bit short notice, isn't it?"

"Yes sir, we need to get this all sorted out, once and for all."

"I think it'll be OK, I'll ring my parents and we'll probably be with you later this afternoon."

George called his mum, who in turn, got hold of Michael. Within a half hour, she called back.

"Hello George."

"Hello mum."

"We're just about to leave. Shall we pick you up?"

"Brilliant, mum. Thank you., see you in a minute."

"As they arrived at the police station, there was a small gathering of news people, hanging around, waiting for any titbits of news from Hetthorpe but Michael negotiated them safely and they managed to park next to the main entrance. They entered the reception, noticing that the door was still in the same shape as when Michael made his last entrance. They also noticed another gathering of reporters in the reception, who, on hearing the door open, turned as one, in the hope of someone bringing news of any sort, to relieve them of their boredom.

"Gilbert family to see Superintendent Nichols." Lilie said to the duty constable. Purposely not mentioning Hetthorpe.

George was feeling nauseous, from the last memory of this place. He was also aware of one particular reporter, who had noticed his limp and was having a good look at his eye, that still carried some swelling and bruising.

"Excuse me sir." She called, grabbing the attention of everyone else.

But she was too late, the duty officer pressed a button which opened the door to his right and they were ushered in by Sergeant Stone.

"Welcome, welcome." greeted Nichols in an artificial gesture of sincerity. "Please take a seat. Tea, coffee?"

"No thanks", Michael answered on behalf of everyone. "Lets get this over and done with, whatever this is."

"I take it, you know everyone here, Sir James," who shook Michael and Georges hands and embraced Cynthia and Lily.

"Hello." he said, in his usual friendly way. "Don't worry yourselves, it's all going to be alright."

Superintendent Nichols turned to two men. One in a two piece pin stripe suit and a plain white shirt, without a tie, the other, in dark blue jeans, and a blue tee shirt, with the police crest over his left breast.

"In the suit." said the superintendent "is PC Jones and the one in the jeans is PC Adams.

Michael felt his blood start to boil but managed to keep calm, while George was shaking uncontrollably. Lilie holding his hand, gently.

"It was suggested that they do this by letter but I felt that doing so would mean nothing to you. It being so easy to write a letter, instead of looking the victim in the eye to apologise. So, now, George. They have something to say to you. Adams?"

Adams stood.

"Mr Gilbert."He began. I sincerely apologise for my actions, that day. I appreciate that we were over the top in our treatment of you, while all you were doing is what you genuinely considered, your bit. I hope that you are getting over your injuries and I wish you well for the future. Please accept my humble apologies."

"Jones." Urged Nichols.

Jones remained seated.

"I too am very sorry, Mr Gilbert."He uttered. "Genuinely, I am sorry for mistreating you and causing you injury. Doing our duty as police officers, in the investigation of a very serious crime, we don't know what to expect and situations can become nasty in a matter of seconds. Unfortunately, you were in the wrong place, at the wrong time. Once again, I apologise."

Michael was fuming, he looked at George, who was astounded at Jones's implication that he had bought it on himself. While Adams did seem genuine, Jones was anything but. Sir James looked disgusted, Nichols sat, head down in disbelief in what he'd just heard.

Nichols finally got up.

"Anything you would like to say, George?"

George shuffled uncomfortably in his seat.

"I accept the apology of PC Adams but certainly not that of PC Jones. In fact, I didn't even recognise what he said as an apology."

In honesty, replied Nichols, "Neither did I." He turned to the officers.

101

"While this enquiry has been going on, I have spoken to my superiors and to your union reps. All have agreed to give me the final decision on your futures and whatever I decide, they will stand by. No doubt your agents would have advised you of this already. Your victim and his family, some reluctantly, have accepted Georges decision not to prosecute. You are very lucky, because I have no doubt that guilty verdicts would have meant imprisonment. Not a good place for a convicted cop. Suspension had been suggested but, as a result of today's arrogance and lack of humility toward your victim, I am dismissing you, Jones, from the force, for gross misconduct, and conduct unbefitting an officer of the law. This is with immediate effect. You don't seem to realise, Jones, that apologies do not come with a BUT and this arrogance leads me to believe that I have made the right decision, regarding yourself"

"Sir?"Jones was clearly stunned.

"You heard me, Jones. You know where the door is."

"I'll sue." Jones retaliated.

"So will I." Shouted George.

Jones stubbornly, remained seated, much to the annoyance of everyone.

"PC Adams," continued Nichols. "You too could have been facing criminal charges. Your willingness to go along with your colleagues actions, smacks of inexperience and naivety. You chose to ignore the protocol of rights, to instead, abet Jones. Maybe it was out of respect for a more experienced officer, I don't know. But, your were complicit in a disgraceful and cowardly assault on an innocent person.

However, to your credit, you have gone along with this enquiry with honesty and integrity. Admitting your failings and have been humble in your apology. You have already spent one week on suspension and, with the families permission, I commit you to a further week of suspension, both weeks, of course without pay or benefits. When you return, if you return, you will be back on a probation period of six months, working closely with sergeant Stone. You will mirror him and do as he says without question. He, in turn, will send me a weekly report on your progress. Is that Clear?"

"Yes sir,, thank you sir." Replied a very relieved Adams, who also mouthed a "thank you", to George.

Jones got up and turned to leave but Michael couldn't hold it in, he stood directly in front of him, looked him in the eye and told him straight.

"There's a reception full of reporters, downstairs, I'm happy to stand in the middle of them, with you and tell them all what you did. Do you fancy that?"

Jones made a feeble attempt to pass but knew it was futile. Michael whispered in Jones's ear.

"This isn't over, for you. The sooner you come back to Hetthorpe, the better." Then, he let him pass, while George pulled his father away. A father who, until recent weeks had never shown a modicum of violence. Georges father, a father George was proud of. His hero.

After both Jones and Adams had left, Nichols asked Michael.

"Where did you park your car, Mr Gilbert?"

"Next to the reception entrance." He replied.

"Do you think the press noticed you?"

"They did have a look but I think they were more looking for your officers. One woman reporter in reception, noticed us and wanted to speak to George."

"Tell you what, lets swap keys, you take my car, out of the pound and I'll get Stone to take your car, then you can meet somewhere in town and swap back. How does that sound?"

"Sounds good to me." Michael agreed.

"Brilliant." said Nichols. "Love a bit of subterfuge. Seriously, to you all and especially George, I apologise. This episode has been an embarrassment to me and the force. I hope you are happy with my actions and I hope that Adams has learned from this. You are a good family, that, in itself, a pleasure to see. Let me wish you all well and may the troubles that are afflicting your lovely village, soon be over, with the children all being safely reunited with their families."

"Thank you,, Claude." Said sir James. Best wishes to you and your family. He turned to the family.

"Shall we go now?"

There was no argument. Another ordeal was over.

19

A full week had passed and by the 10th of August there was still no progress reported by the police. On the plus side, there had been no further abductions but the lack of information and clues left the police in limbo. And the longer it went on, the less confident the whole village was becoming about finding Wendy, Peter and Lucy alive.

Lilie got out of bed and rushed to the toilet, where she was violently sick.

"You alright, my wife?"

"Fine, just been a bit sick, that's all."

"OK, OK. Shall I get the doctor?"

"No. Just go to work, I'll be fine."

"You sure?"

"Go to work, George, I'm alright. Probably something I ate."

"If you're sure. I don't have anything to do down there, it's boring."

"GEORGE!"

"OK. I'm going. See you later."

"Love you, my husband."

But it went unheard, as he shut the door a little heavier than usual.

"Morning George." Shouted Cynthia, as George walked down the path, to the cottage. She was once again, in the garden, secateurs in one hand, dead heads in the other.

"Morning mum." George replied. "Bit early for gardening?"

"The only time I have, with you and your dad, slave driving me." She giggled. I'll be in now. Dad will make you a cuppa."

"Morning dad." George shouted, as he entered the outer door.

"Morning son. Hows you, this morning?"

"I'm alright thanks.. bored but OK. You're on spud harvesting today, aren't you?"

"Yes and before you ask, me and Alec can manage. You just have another week to get right, so don't rush back."

"But Dad."

"But Dad, nothing. There's tea in the pot make yourself busy by pouring up. Where's Lilie?"

"She's home, in a right mood. Been sick and now stroppy. I offered to get her a doctor but she just bit my head off and sent me off to work."

"Who's stroppy?" Asked Cynthia, as she walked in on half the conversation.

"Lilie." snapped George. And he told the story of his morning, so far.

"You men." She stormed.

"What?" the men answered as one, amusing themselves in that fact.

"You know nothing of a womans ways. I've got some paperwork to do first, then I'll pop up to see her."

"I'll go, after my cuppa." said George.

"No. You stay here and help me. it's about time one of you lumps learned something about how this business works."

"Really?"

"Really."

Michael quickly drank his tea and slipped out of the door, casting a sly wink and smile at George, who was bemused by what he'd let himself in for.

*****

"Thank you." Said Lilie, down the phone. I'll be there at eleven."

She'd made an appointment to see the doctor, though she had a pretty good idea what was wrong with her. Or more to the point, what was right with her. She wrote a note for George, apologising for being so tetchy and explained that she had gone to the doctors at Landale, after a little shopping. Further saying that she was fine and that there was nothing to worry about.

It was roughly 0940 when she arrived at the supermarket. There was an aura about her. A good aura. Walking up and down the isles, buying the usual foods and other products, while spending a little more time looking at products that would, soon enough be added to the shopping list. A warm glow enveloped her and she smiled to herself. Thinking about how proud George would be.

But...She had been seen and unbeknown to her, eyes followed her every move. Eyes that were scheming, planning. Eyes that were plotting an agenda.

The shopping done, she quietly walked to the car and placed the two bags in the boot. All happy and not really a care in the world. She steadily drove out of the car park and headed back to Landale and the surgery. There wasn't a lot of traffic around, so she felt relaxed as she made her way along, not noticing the blue van, following her at a reasonable distance away. In fact, itdidn't even draw her attention, as she parked outside the surgery and the van drove slowly by.

Lilie was greeted by the receptionist, Claire Milner. A good friend from school, who comforted Lilie in the aftermath of Georges attack.

"Hello Lilie." She beamed the greeting, with a bright smile and sparkling eyes. "Lovely to see you, even if it's in the doctors. Hope you're OK."

"I'm fine, thank you Claire. In fact, more than fine. What about you and the family?"

"Oh good", Claire replied with that knowing look. "We're all fine too, thanks. Fred has a job, he's a lorry driver for the brewery....... So worried and sad for what's going on in Hettie. Any news on that?"

"No, not yet. It is a worrying time. No abductions for a week, so that's something, at least."

"Well I hope it's all over soon," said Claire. "You're lucky, it's quiet today, so you can go in next. I'll buzz you."

"Thanks Claire."

It was seconds before Lilie actually got into the doctors room. She had picked up a Peoples Friend but was immediately buzzed by Claire, who waved a hurrying hand to Lilie. Once inside, she was greeted by Doctor Green. He was mainly a Landale doctor but could often be seen at Hetthorpe, with the surgery's swapping opening hours.

"Hello Mrs Gilbert. What can we do for you today?"

Lilie explained what had happened in the morning and other things that had not been happening for days prior to the morning.

"Hmmm", the doctor mused. I think, I hope that we both know already, what's going on. Any chance you can provide a little urine?"

"I think I can manage that."

He gave her a little plastic cup, with a small lollipop type of stick.

"You know where the ladies loo is, don't you?"

"Yes." Lily replied and left the room.

She returned and handed the sample to Doctor Green, who smiled.

"I hope it's the result you want, Mrs Gilbert. It looks to me like you're expecting a child."

Lilie almost fainted but the joy overcame her and she cried instead. Smiley tears ran down her face as Doctor green passed her a box of tissues.

"Please make another appointment for tomorrow, with the nurse. Who will take some blood to further confirm what we both already know. I love these occasions. Congratulations Mrs Gilbert. He smiled almost as broadly as Lilie, as he walked her to the door.

As she entered the reception area, she could see that Claire was busy with another patient but caught her eye. Claire raised a questioning thumbs up and Lilie replied with a huge smile, with her thumbs up. Claire, once again beamed her bright smile and waved her arms in the air and mouthed "YAY," much to the other patients confusion. Lilie put a finger to a pursed lip and then a fist to her ear, mimicking a telephone. Claire acknowledged with another thumbs up and Lilie left.

After sitting in the car for a couple of minutes, to compose herself, she pulled away for the short drive home. Within 15 yards, she did notice a blue van close behind her. It did unnerve her, slightly but she assumed that she might have been a little early pulling out on it and even waved an apology in the mirror.

Landale slipped away behind them and they started into the long straight, towards Hetthorpe. The van pulled out to pass but slowed with the passenger window adjacent to Lilies window.

They both slowed down further. Lilie glanced across and had to do a double take. she almost crashed off the road, in shock at what she saw. A little girl, sobbing, pleading.

"Wendy?" Lilie heard herself saying. Then shouting. "WENDY!"

The van then pulled away slightly, getting just in front of Lilie, before turning into a crescent layby, that was shielded by an island of trees. A place that lorry drivers often parked overnight and even in the daytime, for their breaks. It was also just 300 yards short of the first dwellings of Hetthorpe and within half of a mile to home. Lilie felt that she had no choice but to follow the van into the layby. No other vehicle was in there. No-one had stopped for their lunch or even a breakdown. It was just Lily and the blue van.

In seconds a man, wearing a balaclava got to Lilies door. He wrenched it open and grabbed her wrist, pulling her violently.

"Get your shopping."

She obeyed and was then manhandled into the back of the van. Hurting her shins on the way in. Inside, was two more bags of shopping and two children, also crying. Peter Clarke and Lucy Weaver. Both were cruelly bound and gagged with tape Wendy was still in the front seat, cowered down, whimpering. She pulled Peter and Lucy close and gave them the cuddles that they craved, they settled quickly.

"Heads down and if any of you get your head above the window, this one gets hurt." and to make his point, he punched Wendy in the upper arm, causing her to scream, which in turn caused the others to do likewise.

"QUIET." He shouted and as quickly as it started. It stopped. The two in Lilies arms, trembling with fear.

He pulled away quickly and turned right, out of the layby. The sway of the van, told Lilie that he was heading back to Landale. Lilies car was left behind, boot and drivers door open, engine still running a dropped and split milk carton lay on the gravel, it's contents leaking out and trickling down towards the gutter.

*****

108

At around 1230. George and Cynthia stopped their paperwork and chatting and walked up to the village to see Lilie. She hadn't phoned and George felt it better that he didn't phone her, should he antagonise her again. When they got to the house, it was obvious that Lilie wasn't home, no car in the drive. Not unusual. So George let himself and his mum in and went to the kitchen and put the kettle on. He turned to the fridge and saw the note, under a fridge magnet. As he read it, it he called out to his mum.

"It's OK mum, she's gone shopping, before going to the doctors. Eleven o'clock appointment. Probably called in at Louise and Erics place on the way home. Shall I ring them?"

"No, my son, let her have some "mum" time. Hows that kettle?"

George placed the mugs of tea on the breakfast bar and had turned to get the biscuit barrel, when there was a knock on the door.

"I'll get it." Shouted Cynthia.

She opened the door and there stood Sergeant Stone and PC Adams.

"Hello Mrs Gilbert. Is George home?"

"Yes, come in, what is it?"

"We need to speak with George, Mrs Gilbert, can you stay with us?"

The three of them entered the dining room, where George had just put down his tea.

"Hello George." Said Stone. So sorry but I need to talk to you. Have you seen Lilie today?"

"Of course I have, we got up together, why?" Already, George was beginning to fret.

"Was she OK?"

"Yes, she was fine, she was a little tetchy but fine."

"And where is she now George?"

Probably at her mums house. She's been to the doctors and done some shopping. Here, see her note. What's going on?"

"Sit down George", said Adams. "Please, sit down." Cynthia was already sat, chewing on her handkerchief, knowing that bad news was coming.

George sat.

"George, What car and registration, does Lilie drive?" Asked Adams.

George gave them the information.

"Has she crashed? Is she, is she dead?"

"No, she hasn't crashed. I'm afraid, well, we think she's been abducted." Stone replied and continued to tell George about how a lorry driver had pulled into the layby and found Lilies car, door open and engine running. Lilie nowhere to be seen.

"Shall I get the car?" was all that George could think of to say.

"I'm afraid not George. The area is a crime scene and is completely sealed off." Said Adams. George, I owe you and I will do whatever it takes to get your wife back safely to you."

"I'll ring Louise and get her to pop around, said Cynthia. She's just around the corner."

"Would you mind finding Michael for me please?" She asked the officers.

"I'll go." said Adams.

"Better I went said Stone."

George described where his father would be working and Stone left.

*****

They hadn't travelled very far along even road when the van lurched off to the left and slowed considerably as the driver negotiated what were obviously potholes. Branches suddenly screeched down the sides of the van and continued to do so for a couple of minutes, before finally coming to a halt. The driver got out and opened the back door, grabbed Lilie and yanked her out. Before she knew where she was, he covered her head with a small blanket. It stank of heaven knows what but she could discern diesel and even stale cigarettes. He wrapped tape around her wrists and ankles, before pushing her backwards, into the van once more. Then he got the children.

"You know where to go." He ordered. "Go there quietly or you know what will happen. Me and Lilie will be right behind you, any messing and she'll be the first to get hurt?"

"Lilie, you said Lilie. You know me."

"Yes, I know you?" He answered, before throwing her over his shoulder and carrying her into a building. Where once inside, she could feel him turn left and down 6 steps, before walking ahead and dropping her onto a couch. Almost landing on top of one of the children. He then took off the cover and covered Lilies and all the childrens mouths with tape. He also taped the childrens hands behind their backs and their ankles together.

"I'll be back in less than two minutes." And he left, shutting and locking the door. The door that provided the only source of light. Lilie could only wonder how long the children had spent in these conditions. There appeared to be no heat and no covers to keep them warm at night.No water to drink, let alone wash with. As for sanitation, there must have been a toilet, or he might have taken them outside for nature, because there was no acrid sewage smells.

After a short time, her eyes became accustomed to dark and she could make out shapes. She realised that all four of them were sharing the couch. There was, what she thought, an arm chair opposite them. Maybe that's where he sat and slept.

"My God. What is to become of us?" She thought.

Then, he returned. Bringing all the shopping with him.

"We got lucky today, kids. Off to another hideout and who do I see, when I went go get some food? Yes, the one and only Lilie Batten. Or is it Gilbert?" He shone a torch onto her hands. "Oh. Wedding and matching engagement rings, very smart. White gold too, no doubt. Very expensive."He took them from Lilies fingers ripping the skin as he did so.

"So you married the farm boy then?"

"Farm boy? Who used to call George, farm boy?" Lilie wondered.

"Mary. Mary Smith. Oh god, it's John Smith." She panicked for a moment and struggled in vain.

"You've worked it out, haven't you? Mrs Farm girl. No. Would it be Mrs Farm Girl, or Mrs Farm Boy? I don't know. I don't really care."

Suddenly, he reached over and backhanded Lilies face.

"Dreamed of doing that, ever since the court days. *I love you, George*, he sneered. Remember saying that, in the middle of the court, so everyone could hear? I do. He might have gone to Mary, had you not been in the way. Look at me, I went to prison and Mary, along with her alcoholic dad and her control freak mum, put as much distance between themselves and me as they could. All because of you." Then off he went, on a complete tangent.

"Anyway, kids. I'd already got some shopping and Mrs Farm, yes, that'll do. Mrs Farm was getting some too. Now we have twice as much. We'll have to eat some stuff quickly, before it goes off, so we get fat, then go on a diet." And he giggled. She'd never heard him laugh but his giggle, more of a cackle. It was awful.

After searching around in Lilies bags, he found her purse. Shinning his torch on it, he opened it.

"Blimey kids, we're rich. Bank cards, credit cards. Look, cash. Though only he could see it. Fifty quid. We don't need another hide out, we can stay here. We can be a family. Your my kids and she's your mummy."

After over one hour of ramblings about family, he remembered something.

"Here, darling wife. When I followed you, you went to the doctors. Why was that then?" Lilie started to weep. He didn't see it, he only noticed when she sniffled. "Come on, tell us. Silly me, you've still got tape on. Lilie turned away, as he he reached to pull the tape off. He stopped and shone his light on something. A gun. A small one but a gun nonetheless.

"I'm going to take your tapes off, so you can eat. Scream or shout, or try anything stupid, a child dies, Understood?"

Everyone rapidly nodded their heads. He left their legs taped but gave them the freedom to move there arms, and indeed, eat. Lilie was the last to be semi released.

"Now then, my new wife, why were you at the doctors? You don't look ill. In fact, you look great. Come on, he whispered menacingly in her ear, with the gun trained on her temple. Tell me. TELL ME." The click of the gun hammer scared her.

"I'm. I'm."

"Come on." he growled, pushing the gun harder into her head.

"I'm having a baby, I'm pregnant, she shouted. Then whispered, Georges baby."

"Hear that kids? we're having a baby. What great news." He looked in Lilies eyes. "You just saved another kiddie from Hetthorpe. I was going to take another one tonight. A boy, to square it all up. Now, I'm still going to have a mummy AND four kids. That's what Mary wanted, you know, two girls and two boys. Maybe we can send her photographs, once I can find out where she lives."

Later, they ate cooked chicken and crisps. Smith felt he was treating them, with fizzy drinks and chocolate but it was hardly nourishing food. Lilie knew it and was frustrated because she could do nothing. She did have some bananas, in her bag but Smith didn't seem interested. Anything would do.

After the food, he taped all their mouths and hands again but he individually freed their legs to take them, one at a time, for a toilet trip, outside. The last to go was Lilie. She had to have the cover placed over her head, in case she recognised her surroundings. Once back inside he retreated to what was that old armchair but not before locking the door and putting the key in his pocket.

No sleep was had that night, for Lilie. The poor children did get fitful sleeps but they had lived this way for a long, long week. They were so tired and weak, after such a long and trying ordeal, an ordeal that none of them could see an end to. Perhaps Lilies presence gave them some comfort and hope, thus helping them to get some sleep, however fitful.

Lilie wept, silently. She was helpless. Smith was obviously demented and his ramblings worried her more and more. What was he planning? Was he going to keep them, even after Lilies baby is born? Was this hovel their future? No matter what he was planning, there was nothing Lilie could do without jeopardising the childrens lives.

She watched Smiths silhouette and listened to him snore. He seemed to sleep as soundly as if he was at home. Relaxed, not a care in the world. A man with a plan.

*****

113

Sergeant Stone and PC Adams worked hard, after leaving George and Lilies home. They visited the layby and studied tyre marks in the gravel. They were also drawn to an area of loose gravel, that contained footprints. Three sets. There was one of a male boot. Deep tread, like a heavy work boot and about a size ten. It appeared to be dragged to one side, while two smaller prints suggested ladies' plimsolls, both appeared to be dragged and both in the same direction of the male boot print. Finally, there were two very light footprints. Definitely the size and shape of a childs sandal. There was a damp area in between the prints, which, after a small area, ran off into a line, in the same direction as the prints. Stone assumed a direction and carefully walked a few feet towards the end of the layby and noticed that the ladies size stopped and were seen no more. Where the child prints went to the left and into the short grass, followed by clear left and right boot prints. The child prints stopped after a mere four feet but the boots continued, before turning right and out of loose gravel. Adams had found the milk carton, that had found it's way into the grass. Whether by the wind, or some scavenging animal. The carton was obviously new and the price label was from "Kwik Buy".

Stone called the white coated scientists over and while they took samples and photographs of virtually everything, he and Adams walked slowly and stooped, to the end of the layby. Two nearside tyre tracks cut into the grass and seemed to suddenly veer off to the right, the rear one appeared to fish tail a little.

"They've gone Landale way."He mused, rubbing his chin. He was exited. At last, a breakthrough. Albeit at the expense of Lilies's safety.

"There was child, I'm certain of it." He said. Red faced and with the hairs on the back of his neck standing on end. "What do you think, Adams?"

"Well, serge. If there was one child, it means that, if this our man, at least one child is still alive."

"Quite right, Adams, quite right. Come on. We're off to Kwik Buy. Time is of the essence."

They draughted in two more uniformed officers to assist. All till assistants were questioned and shown a photograph, that

George had earlier provided. Two recognised Lilie and one even produced a copy of what probably was Lilies's till receipt, which among other items listed, were two cartons of milk. More importantly was the time of the receipt.

Next stop was back into Landale and the doctors surgery, where they were greeted by Claire and her beaming smile, even though she was unnecessarily nervous by their arrival.

"Hello, young lady." Adams introduced himself. "And this is Sergeant Stone. We're conducting a missing person enquiry. Do you recognise this lady?" He produced Lilies picture.

Claire gasped and put her hand up to her mouth, as her eyes filled with stinging tears.

"Missing? Lilies missing?? She was here this morning.

"You obviously know her." Adams continued.

"We were friends at school. What's happened?"

"I'm sorry to say, It looks like she has been abducted" added Stone.

Claire gave all the information she could, without giving away Lilies's secret. She was in shock and distraught but did the best she could.

"Did you see her leave?" Asked Adams.

"Yes, I watched her drive away."

"And did you see, or notice anything, what the traffic was like, was she followed?"

"No, I don't think so. A dark blue van came up behind her and I saw her wave, so thought she knew him, the driver."

"You're sure it was a male driver?"

"Definitely, they slowed down a little and I could easily see. I even thought I recognised him. Oh, he had a little girl with him. It looked almost as though she was sat on his knee."

"Thank you, Claire. We might have to speak to you again."

"No problem, please find her safe and well."

"We are trying, believe me."

As they left, Stone suggested that they go back to the supermarket.

"Why serge."

"A hunch, Adams, just a hunch?"

They found the lady that produced the receipt, she was getting ready to go home.

"Thank you for your time, already." Said Stone. "Just a few more questions."

"Did anyone else catch your eye? A stranger perhaps? Came in a blue van."

"Well yes, actually. I saw them turn up."

"Them?" asked Adams.

"A scruffy man and a little girl. He put her in the back, before coming into the shop."

"Can you describe the either of them?" Stone demanded, irritably.

"Not the little girl, she was just that bit too far away but I served the man. Smelled a bit too. Shall I try to find his till receipt?"

"That would be an idea." Snapped Stone.

And she walked away to the office.

"You alright sergeant?" Asked Adams.

"Three kids, missing from a village not too far from here and the whole world knows about it. She sees a scruffy man shove a little girl into the back of a van and doesn't call the police?? Disgusting and there's nothing I can do about it. She'd better hope that we find them alive. I'll risk my career to shame her."

She returned with the receipt and they read through it. Various items, including cooked chicken and fizzy drinks. To Stone, it was all adding up.

"You were going to give a description of the man." Adams reminded her.

She gave a perfect description of John Smith, Complete with the scar over his right eye.

"Thank you, you've been very helpful."Said Stone, somewhat unconvincingly.

"I need a telephone." Said Stone And went to the office, relieving the manager of his office. He was gone for almost fifteen minutes when "WHAT!" Reverberated around the store. Stone emerged two minutes later crimson and shaking with rage.

"Sergeant?"

"We have a problem. Adams". He related the history of John Smith. "A judge sentences him to twelve years. All to be served

116

in maximum security. Six years later, the do gooders get him into a soft, open prison and what does he do? He walks, simply walks. Unbelievable. Nobody at our division were notified and now we have a very dangerous man on the loose. It's probably him that's got the children and Lilie.

"Radio in what we have, Adams. And get them to put an alert on a blue van. Make and registration details not known."

"Actually, serge, I radioed that bit, while you were in the office."

"Well done lad. Pity anyone that drives a blue van. They're all going to get stopped, or visited."

20

Lilie saw a bit of light, trying to get through the gap at the bottom of the door and the cold stone floor. It was so quiet. She wondered where they could be. The journey from the layby to this awful place, didn't take long, so they must be at an isolated place, on the outskirts of Landale. A derelict farm, perhaps. Thoughts ran through her mind, Did she know of any such place, outside of Landale? Nothing would come.

Smith stirred. It wasn't pitch black but still very dark in that cellar, or whatever it was but he could see enough to do a head count.

"Good, four people, still here. I hope you slept well. I'm going out soon, so I'll let you eat and then I'll take you to do your toilet thing first. Any complaints?" Lilie almost let out an incredulous laugh, at such a mad question. Maybe as well she was gagged, preventing her from doing so.

After a breakfast of more cooked chicken and crisps, washed down by the second carton of Lilies's milk, he taped their legs and arms again. The childrens's mouths were sore from constant placing and removing of the tape. Each removal taking a little skin, infection was inevitable. Lilie herself was already feeling sore and realised what the children were going through. So before he taped her mouth, she pleaded with him, explaining what would be happening. She tried to get him on her side.

"Look". She said, calmly. "It's no good us bringing up children with infections. They could die and it would have all been for nothing."

"Good thinking."He said. Lilie more expected another backhander than a reasonable answer. "But how will I keep you all quiet?"

"Take my money and get some Vaseline, to rub around their mouths. Please get some water too, so I can clean them up a little. Maybe some soap, basic hygiene. We must look after our kids, you know. You could get some cotton wool too, that could do as gagging, as well as cleaning. I mean the gags aren't on that long and its the glue on the tape that causing the problem."

She stopped, worried that she was pushing him too hard. He was quiet, thinking, considering.

"You're absolutely right." He suddenly exclaimed. "I'll have to put the tape on this time but yes, I'll get all those things. I'll get bandages too. Lots of them for tying and for injuries. You're clever, Lilie. I'm glad we're together."

So he once again, bound and gagged everyone and, incredibly, kissed each one of them, including Lilie, on the forehead, before bidding a cheerful farewell. Just as any loving father/husband would, as he leaves to go to work, or to the pub but still, locking the door as he left. His happy whistle, fading, as he got further away.

*****

It was a nice day but and he'd left happily enough but his mood was being tested, as he drove down the track, bouncing and scraping the trees, the continued scraping grating on his nerve ends, he could feel his mood changing. The whistling had stopped and was replaced with profanities as he twisted and jerked along the track. Finally, to give him something else to think about, he turned the radio on and one of his favourite songs "Philadelphia Freedom, by Elton John was almost finished. It calmed him down, a little and it even got him singing. He'd liked the song as a twelve year old, though freedom was far from a consideration that he was giving, for his captives.

The song finished and after a couple of local adverts, it was news time. He got some sick pleasure from listening to the local news. To him, he had celebrity status but it had gone off the boil for a day or two, with no-one getting any closer to finding him, or the children. However, the taking of Lilie was to rekindle the public's fire of loathing of him and his status would be restored, even though he would have to rethink any plans that he'd had for his captives.

Almost at the end of the bumpy track, he stopped and turned up the volume.

"Good morning. It's nine o'clock and this is your news, from your local station." A voice announced. "Reaching out to

119

all of the Kirklees districts, including you, in the Spen Valley. Followed by forced laughter from the announcer.

"Get on with it." growled Smith.

"The abductions of the Hetthorpe children, took another twist, last night. A popular and well known lady was taken, shortly after visiting her doctor in Landale. Lilie Gilbert, 20, wife of George Gilbert and daughter of Louise and Eric Batten, had been shopping, then visited her doctor. She was seen to leave the doctors and headed out towards Hetthorpe but, for some reason had pulled into the layby, just short of the village. The police confirm that there were signs of a struggle and tracks suggest that the abductor then drove off back in the direction of Landale. Police also confirm that a blue van was seen by three different people, within the time frame that Lilie was taken.. Here's more from our reporter."

"Good morning. Yes, I have with me an officer from Huddersfield Central.

"Sergeant Stone….."

"Him..." Smith shouted at the radio.

"What can you tell us about the blue van?"

"Well", answered Stone. There is no make to report on the van, or a registration number. A child was seen, on two different occasions, in this van and this same van was also seen to be directly behind Lilies car, as she left Landale. It is imperative that we find this van. It is described as being of a royal blue and it is further suggested that it could be of the Transit size, or type. If you have a friend or neighbour that has such a vehicle, or even know someone that drives one of these for a living, contact us. All calls are deemed as confidential and we won't ask for your name. Thank you."

"Is there anything else, Sergeant?"

"Yes, there is." We have a possible identification of the driver." Stone bowed his head. "The driver has been identified as John Smith. He escaped from an open prison, two weeks ago, where he was serving time for GBH with intent. If you see this van, if you see him, do not approach, he is a very dangerous individual. Telephone us immediately. Thank you." And he shuffled off. It was a gamble, giving Smiths name etcetera. It would certainly panic the families of his captives but he felt that it would protect the rest of the community and give them something, or someone to look out for.

"Thank you Sergeant Stone," The reporter said, to Stones departing back. "Lets hope that there can be a happy ending to this awful drama, quite soon. Back to the Studio."

"Indeed." Said the presenter. "I and the whole of the world, probably echo those sentiments…... In other news."

Smith turned off the radio. He was excited.

"They know it's me, he, heee." he cackled that giggle, while rubbing his hands together. "But I don't answer to Smith!! Come on. Come and get me, he shouted." For no-one to hear.

He drove to the main road and turned around, going back to the hideout. No temper, just a calm slow drive.

"No hurry." He thought. "I'll have to walk to find another vehicle."

When he stopped, he fumbled around in the glove box and found his pen knife, which he used to remove the number plates. His thinking was that it would waste more of the polices time, tracing the owner. Should they come this way.

On his walk from the derelict building, he felt it would be good to tell his family what he was doing. So he returned. Not opening the door, he banged, frightening all inside and shouted.

"Sorry, darlings, I'm going to be later than expected. Something came up." It made him feel good, letting them know what he was doing and, as he left, he started whistling again, with a gravely voiced "Philadelphia Freedom," happily piercing the air.

*****

Instead of calling at Landale, he walked for another mile or so, to the outskirts of Huddersfield and found another supermarket. Buying as many antiseptic creams as he dared. He bought bandages and cotton wool. He genuinely thought that he was being ingenious and caring, buying sanitary towels and pads to use as gags.

Other shoppers looked at him in disgust, avoiding him. Not that they recognised him, it was the smell. Becoming aware that he was being looked at, with repugnance, he decided that he was attracting too much attention, so he went to the till to pay.

121

"Would you like a bag, sir?" Asked the young cashier. Lily, on her name badge.

"I reckon, Lily. That's my wifes name, only spelt different.

"Lots of bandages." She said, nervously.

"St John stuff." he replied. Can we get a move on?

"Sorry sir."

Smith bagged his purchases and grabbed his change, not noticing the girl pressing a button under the counter.

Feeling uncomfortable, he walked away quickly, looking around. A siren in the distance made him freeze for a second, then two sirens. A third, getting closer. Almost panicking, befroe realising that it was giving him a buzz, as ducked into a side street, a service road for street side shops. No-one saw him, all eyes were on the blue lights, heading towards them and in the direction of the supermarket. He composed himself and realised that he needed to get away quickly. He walked, almost ran around a corner and, while looking backwards bumped into a man, in his forties, knocking both of them to the floor.

"Steady." Shouted Brian Noble. An independent baker, he'd just locked his shop and was coming out of the back entrance, when Smith bowled him over.

"Idiot, watch what you're doing." As he raised himself up.

Smith reacted in the only way he knew how. He also rose, simultaneously hitting Mr Noble under the chin, causing him to rise up, then fall backwards, falling, until the back of his head hit the edge of the kerb. Unconsciousness was instant, death was not far behind.

Firstly confused, Smith pulled himself together and looked at Mr Noble, then kicked him hard in the ribs, as if to confirm what he had done. Looking around, he saw keys, a bag and scattered change. He grabbed the keys and looked in the bag, which contained the days takings. No time to count but he considered that there were enough notes for him not to worry about the loose change on the road. Finally, he located a white Volkswagen van. No sign writing and a push on the fob cancelled the alarms system and allowed entry. It was working out alright for Smith. Inside the van, there was a white coat and a straw hat, the type that bakers would wear. He donned those, although the coat was a little tight. As he started up, he looked

122

over his shoulder and saw that there were two wicker baskets, full of bread, fresh bread. He thought it was strange how he'd not noticed the smell before. Although he did feel charmed and happy that his family would eat good food tonight and that they had new transport. As he passed the body of Brian Noble, he looked down and simply said.

"Unlucky."

The main street that he'd ducked away from, was full of people looking away from Smith and towards the supermarket, where hoards of police were out, inspecting every piece of ground within. Interviewing and getting nowhere. He turned left, driving away unnoticed by anyone. It would be a long time before Mr Noble would be found.

*****

Using the side roads and country lanes, it took Smith longer than planned to get finally back to his hideout. Dusk was arriving quickly, which suited him but was terrible for his captives. All had been cooped up in their hovel, gagged and tied, for over 10 hours. All had soiled themselves and Wendy, especially had badly soiled. She was sweating profusely, the beads reflecting from the fading sun that had found its way into their darkness.

"Lilie, I'm going to free you, to look at Wendy. Try anything stupid and you both die. UNDERSTAND?"

He was menacing. Frightened or angry, Lilie didn't know either way but she nodded her head vigorously.

"Please, some water." As he took the gag off.

Luckily, there was plenty left from Lilies shopping, he had forgotten to buy some, in his haste to get out of the supermarket. He threw a small bottle at her and it landed on the sofa, where she had been sat. splashing in her own waste.

"We are not going to survive this." She thought out loud.

"You will, if and only if, you behave." Stormed Smith.

Lily pulled the tape from Wendys mouth, only to be met with a flood of vomit. Lilie washed it away, quickly and washed Wendys mouth.

"I need light, I can't see what's wrong. Get us out, she screamed."

123

"Don't shout at me." Smith retorted. "I'm in charge here."

Lilie swooped Wendy up into her arms.

"Well your going to have to shoot both of us because I am taking Wendy out of that door. Right now!!"

She braced herself, as she barged passed him and carried Wendy out into the fading sunlight, where she stopped and sat Wendy on the top step. No gunshots and no more shouting.

As Lilie bathed Wendy's mouth, she noticed that the blisters were turning septic, yellow puss almost ran down her chin, while some went into her mouth.

Calmly, Lilie asked.

"Did you get any antiseptics?"

"Yes." he meekly replied. "Plenty. As he handed her the bag with everything he'd bought.

"Wendy." Lily whispered. "This is going to sting, I'm so sorry but I have to wash the nasties out from around your mouth. Is that OK?"

Wendy nodded.

"There's a brave girl."

As she worked she dared to ask Smith.

"John. Please take off the tape from Peter and Lucy's mouths and wash them, like I'm doing. You'll be good won't you, children?"

They both nodded.

Smith didn't move for a few seconds. He couldn't believe that he let anyone tell him what to do.

"John." Lilie snapped. "Look, these things aren't very nice but it's what you have to do when you have a family. OK?"

He grunted and did as he was told. Even rubbing Peters hair, as he got to him.

When Lilie had done all that she could for Wendy, she went over to help Smith.

"I see you got plenty of bandages, which is good. Perhaps we can take the tape off the childrens's legs and arms and then we can clean them up......."

"Yes, yes, yes." Said Smith. "That was my plan."

"Why the sanitary towels?" She asked.

"Gags, of course, Better then tape."

"She was almost impressed. Almost.

"We can't go back in there." Smith admitted. "It's germ infested now. "I've got a new van, we'll sleep in the blue one tonight and leave here tomorrow, in the new one and find somewhere more suitable."

"OK." Said Lilie. Though the thought of something more suitable didn't fill her with any enthusiasm. Apart from the children, all that was on her mind was George. How was he, was he coping?

"I miss you and love you, my husband, be brave and strong." She whispered to herself, while Smith was out of earshot.

Unfortunately, George was struggling. He was missing Lilie badly and was making himself angry and frightened at the same time. He didn't know he could feel the anger that he was feeling. But twice, Smith had blighted his life and the rage inside himself was building. He'd made a vow to himself, to find Smith and put paid to him once and for all. But Lilie, his darling wife, Lilie was, right now at Smiths mercy. Getting her home safe comes first.

"I love you, my wife." he said, over and over, while keeping a vigil at the spot where Lilie was taken.

*****

The last of the children, bound and gagged. Smith was about to lift Wendy into the back of the van. When all of a sudden, she dropped to the floor and started to fit. Going rigid, then shaking uncontrollably.

"Get her gag off!" Lilie screamed. "Get it off, she's convulsing."

"Don't you think I know that, you stupid woman?" He shouted, while giving her one more backhand across the face.

He then reached down and took the gag from Wendys mouth. Only to be met with a mouthful of vomit. She was still fitting but all he wanted to do was hit her.

"No!" Screamed Lilie, as she barged Smith out of the way. Preventing him from hitting the stricken Wendy.

Lilie picked up Wendy and held her tight, hushing her, kissing her forehead, as she slowly but surely eased down from her convulsions.

125

"She'd dying, John." Lilie sobbed. She's dying. We must get her to the hospital."

"Are you mad? The whole of the country is waiting for me to make one mistake and it's all over, for me. And you, WIFE!"

"No, John." Lilie pleaded. We can drop her off somewhere and then phone the police to come and get her."

"Who's going to speak to them? You, I suppose. They'll get me for sure."

"Not if we do it right." Lilie was thinking fast.

"Think about it John, please. We find a phone box, close to the hospital. I make the 999 call, with you beside me. I tell whoever answers, what to do. We could even leave Wendy in that phone box."

He cooled down and was considering it.

"You won't try to run, or give me away?"

"Why would I? We still have Peter and Lucy to care for. If you want, you could get another one. Don't forget, I'm pregnant, that would be the four that you want."

"True, very true. Come on then, lets go. We don't have much time."

His madness knew no bounds. He was giving up Wendy, with the prospect of snatching another child, while being prepared to wait for almost eight months for Lilie to give birth. Lilie despaired.

They transferred everyone from the blue van, to the new white one and set off. He drove, at speed, risking whatever police might be around but as far as he was concerned, they were looking for a blue van, not a white one. Even though the registration number wouldn't match up with a white van. In what felt like forever they found themselves in an industrial area, at the back of the hospital. They soon found a telephone box, in a street where street lights not only provided light but they also provided shadow. Smith parked in a shadow, as close to the telephone box as he could.

"Keep still and quiet, you two. We won't be long. Say goodbye to Wendy." Stifled and desperate muffles were the only reply.

Gun in his hand and Lilie carrying Wendy, they set off.

Lilie dialled 999.

126

"Emergency, which service please?"

"You need to listen very carefully. My name is Lilie. Wendy Marsden is sick, she is being left in this telephone box. You must come quick."

"Can you give me some mo....?"

"The telephone box is on the industrial area right behind Huddersfield General Infirmary."

Smith cut the phone off.

"Come on, now."

Lilie bent over and quickly cuddled Wendy.

"Bye bye, Wendy. Take care and give my love to mummy and daddy."

If Wendy answered, it went unheard because Smith pulled Lilie backwards, by the hair and dragged her away.

"Come on, now." He snarled.

But instead of getting upset, Lilie thanked him.

"That was very brave of you, to risk getting caught in saving Wendy, very brave. Thank you."

He said nothing. He just drove away, steadily. Not for the first time that day, he heard sirens and saw blue lights light the sky. It still gave him a thrill, being that one step ahead. Maybe this time, it wasn't about him. Maybe someone will live because of them.

*****

It was almost 1115pm. George was still fully dressed but laying, wide awake on his bed. The curtains were open and he could see lights coming over the hill towards his house. They were coming fast. Then suddenly, they stopped, right outside of his house. Next there was a loud banging on his door. Excited, or angry banging, he didn't know but he still ran down the stairs, anticipating what? He didn't know. The door was no sooner off the latch, when the caller burst in, it was PC Adams.

"So sorry to barge in, George. I'm so excited to tell you. We are certain that Lilie is still alive."

"What, really?" George struggled to take it in, as Adams told him all that he knew.

"Lilies chances of remaining alive have increased tenfold, George. If he was going to kill her, he would have done it by now."

127

"Is Wendy alright?" George asked, embarrassed having not already asked.

"She's got a touch of Septicemia, George. It's not great news but she's in good hands. The doctors are confident of a full recovery. Any later getting to hospital would have been different and could certainly have killed her. Now though, Sergeant Stone is probably with her and her parents. She's with the right people."

"I wish Lilie was."

"Just a matter of time, George. I'm certain of it. Listen. Do you want me to go and tell your mum and dad, or me to come with you, for you to tell them?"

"Erm. No, neither, thank you so very much. I'll walk down. Clear my head a little.

They would never have thought it could happen but George and Adams, stood on Georges doorstep and shared a warm handshake. It was a good moment, even though there was still a long way to go.

*****

As they neared the track, for "home", the night revealed lights in their sky. More blue lights for Smith to celebrate, coming from over the trees, lots of blue flashing lights. Beyond those trees, was their prison.

"Every cloud." Said Smith.

"What do you mean?" Asked Lilie.

"If we hadn't have taken Wendy to hospital, we would have been there. That would have been interesting."

"Interesting?"

"Of course. I'm not going quietly. They'll have to take me out. That would be after I'd dealt with you and the kids."

Lilie didn't like to ask what he meant but knew it wasn't good. She gulped.

"All our supplies were there, food, water antiseptics etcetera." She said, hoping to change the subject.

"Yes, well I thought of that and picked up most of it. I need bandages to tie you up." He cackled. "As far as foods concerned. Can't you smell the bread? There's heaps of it back there. It was a bakers van.

"Really? What bakers?"

"Just down the road from a supermarket, outside of Huddersfield."

"You stole it?"

"Of course. I didn't go out and buy it, did I? Besides, the owner didn't need it any more."

"Why?"

"Why do you think Lilie? God you're so naive."

She went quiet again. The truth coming back about why she was here and the madman that she was having to cope with. Where there was a sense of relief that they'd got Wendy to safety, the reality remained that this man was totally unbalanced and could change with the snap of a finger. She realised, right there and then, that she was not still not safe and neither were Peter and Lucy.

Lights were emerging from the track that Smith had become accustomed to. Not blue lights, just full on headlights. The vehicle turning towards them, shone those lights into his cab. It was an ambulance.

"Just saved you a job and you dazzle me..idiot." Then he giggled and blasted the horn, as they passed each other. Not realising that the blast had possibly attracted attention that he could ill afford.

"Two twenty seven to base." radioed the driver.

"Come in two twenty seven."

"Confirming that we have left the police scene. No casualties to report."

"OK. Return to base please."

"En route. Oh. The police have confirmed that the blue van is the one they've been looking for, in connection with the Hetthorpe abductions. Does anyone know what sort of vehicle was stolen from the late Mr Noble?"

"Yes, I believe it's a white Volkswagen van. Why?"

"A white van blasted his horn at us, as we pulled out of the track. Can't confirm the make but can confirm that the driver was male and had a female passenger."They looked to be heading for Landale."

"Brilliant, I'll pass that on. Over and out."

129

*****

"Come on then." Said Smith. "lets find a parking place, for the night. Any suggestions?"

"No, not really." Lilie answered, quietly.

"I know just the place." Smith said, menacingly.

"Where?"

"You'll see, maybe. Now, climb in the back and start tying your ankles together and sort yourself a gag."

"There's no need." She pleaded. "I've done as I've been told, all along. I've even helped you."

"Do as you're told again then and get in the back!"

Peter and Lucy's screams were muffled as they saw Smith backhand Lilie again but this time, instinct made time for Lilie to duck her head and although it hurt, It hurt Smith too, the back of his hand hitting Lilies skull a glancing blow, almost dislocating his little finger. He almost lost control of the van, as he shook his hand in pain.

"For the last time...IN THE BACK!"

Lilie obeyed, quietly. She got in between Peter and Lucy and held them and they all wept together.

They reached the layby where Lilies ordeal began. At the entrance was a square, yellow sign, with black lettering.

INCIDENT HERE, 10/08/1983. DID YOU SEE ANYTHING. CONTACT W YORKS POLICE 01484 836999.

"Yeah, yeah, yeah." Smith snarled, as he knocked the sign over, flattening it.

He stopped and climbed into the back of the van, standing on Lucy as he did so, spraining her ankle. Surprisingly, he apologised, rubbed the ankle, gently and poured some water onto it, before drying it and tightly bandaging it, for support. Lilie was impressed with his apparent expertise and told him so.

"You learn quite a lot of things inside." He growled back.

He turned to Lilie and started to bind her.

"What's wrong?"She asked, quietly, hoping he'd change his mind and keep her unbound.

"You know, only too well."

"I don't. All I know is that we'd crossed a bridge and were making progress, with trust."

130

"NO! You crossed a line. I was trusting you. I did as you wanted and took Wendy to hospital, a massive risk to me. All you did, was draw attention to yourself by giving your name and try to drag out the call time and then tried to gain some more time, by hugging and kissing Wendy. Sending coded messages. "*Give my love to Mummy and Daddy.*" he mocked. Might just as well have told her to give your love to farm boy, George. No, my trust in you is done."

"It wasn't like that." She pleaded.

Smith reached up violently and grabbed Lilie by the chin. His thumb and index finger, painfully forcing her mouth open. His rank breath and spittle, entering her mouth as he ranted and raved about what he would do, should she disobey him again, or try to undermine him.

"So now, you shut up and speak only when I ask you to.. Understand?"

She couldn't reply. All she could do was stare at his insane eyes. She was frozen with fear. He'd accused her of crossing a line. It appeared to Lilie, that he had also crossed a line. Where she thought there might be reason within him, something had taken it away.

*****

Meanwhile, the police dispatched another two crew car. Their brief was to be on the look out for a white Volkswagen van, in the Landale area.The original registration was given but they were warned that the registration plates could have been changed. They were further advised not to approach but to observe, if possible and report anything they see.

Driving, was a new recruit in her first week of service. WPC Allison Treacher had moved to Huddersfield, simply for her career. Born and bred in Carlisle, she'd tried further education, with mixed results but her heart had always been set on joining the police force and, with her parents' misgivings finally but reluctantly exhausted, they gave their blessing. She took the first opportunity that came up and went to Huddersfield. She was ambitious and had set her sights high, taking her role very seriously and followed orders fastidiously. Her parents thought and hoped that maybe that ambition would bear fruit and she would not be so close to the firing line for too long.

Her colleague, Desmond Ingram, was not too different. Young and ambitious but with two years under his belt had caught the eye of Sergeant Stone, who was always keen to promote new and young talent and a report was already being considered by Superintendent Nichols. He was local to the Kirklees district, having been born in Mirfield. Unlike Allison, he was encouraged to join the force. In school, he was seen as a peacemaker. Unable to be rolled over, he did see reason and looked at both sides of an argument before acting for what he felt, was right.

Allison and Desmond were gelling well, for such a short time together. Both already knew when to make a joke and when to shut up. And that's how it was, as they spent almost two hours, quietly driving around Landale, searching areas, including country lanes and industrial sites. All to no avail.

"Shall we stretch our search out a little?" Suggested Des.

"Certainly." Agreed Allison. "Better radio it in though."

"PC Ingram to Central."He mockingly squirmed at Allison.

"Go ahead, Des."

"We've searched high and low, around Landale. Nothing doing, all quiet. Can we extend, towards Hetthorpe, perhaps?"

"By all means. Just give it one more hour, radio in after that and I'll send a replacement crew. Then you two can go home."

"Roger. Over and out."

"*Roger, over and out.*" Allison teased as the headed out toward Hetthorpe.

They drove up and down the lanes that shoot off the main Landale to Hetthorpe route, looking everywhere. Shining torch light into fields of black night, sometimes startling a cow, or a sheep or two. Otherwise, nothing. Until they reached the final layby. As Allison steered in, red reflectors shone, in the night. A white van. Allison crawled the car forward, gently.

"Just a little closer, Alli. I'll radio in."

But, before She'd stopped and before Des could press the mic button, a knock on the passenger window. Allison instinctively stopped the car and Des, just as Instinctively, wound the window down. A voice, quiet and calm, asked.

"You looking for me?"

"Who?" Des started, before a sharp Crack, broke the nights silence. Smiths small gun doing the same work a larger one could do. Snuffing out the life of PC Desmond Ingram in a second. Robbing a wife of a husband and a mother and father of a son.

It didn't stop there. Allison, muted by shock, shaking, no sound coming from her voice as she tried to plead, knew that she was next. Mercifully, it was fast. CRACK! Another innocent victim of John Smiths reign of terror. Her parents were to rue the day that they finally caved in and allowed their precious, one and only child, to follow her dream.

While PCs Treacher and Ingram lay slumped against each other, in a macabre embrace of death, Smith calmly got into the van and started it up. He turned the interior lights on and looked back. Lilie was screaming into her gag, almost choking on the pad. She was aware that he'd shot at something as the shots echoed and the smell of nitroglycerine filled the night air, following him into the van.

"Quiet!!" He shouted and waved the gun, finally pointing at Peter.

"Just two nosey cops, gone off duty. Always better to be a dead hero, than a live one. He found that funny, and cackled, as he drove them all away from the layby.

He turned the radio on. Where he and Lilie both heard that a baker had been killed, while being robbed of his takings and his white van. They also heard that a person, out walking their dog, accidentally came across the blue van, at a derelict farm. They both knew that the net was tightening.

"Looks like show time is coming, Mrs Farm. We're famous."

21

Almost 0430 on Friday the 12th of August, 1983. George was awake, after a few short hours of tossing and turning. The summer was marching on and daybreak was getting substantially later each day, so as darkness remained, George lay on his back, looking at the ceiling, the oncoming daylight trying to make different shapes and shades. Once again, lights caught his attention. Unlike the last time this happened, when it was PC Adams, arriving in a hurry, to bring some good news, the vehicle passed Georges house steadily, not stopping. He didn't get up, to see where it was going, or even to note the type of vehicle, he just lay there, worrying and had never felt so alone in his life.

Eventually, he did get up and went downstairs to make a cup of tea. He turned on the radio, to hear the voice of Mark Collins.

"This has been Mark Collins, with the really early breakfast show. After the news, Barry Crago will be along with the not so really early breakfast show." Have a lovely day and may the sun shine on you."

Advertisements came and went and the usual fanfare introduced the news.

"It's five in the morning and here is your local, national and international news. Good Morning."

"Breaking news. In the early hours of this morning, a police car was found in a layby, just outside Hetthorpe. Two bodies, thought to be those of the officers, were found inside. It is thought they had been shot. No more details are available, as yet, except to say, it is thought that the layby is the same layby that Mrs Lilie Gilbert, from Hetthorpe was snatched."

George turned the radio off. He was furious with himself. That night was the first night that he hadn't kept a vigil, in that layby. He had mental arguments about what would have happened had he been there. Would Smith had killed all his captives had George confronted him, or would he simply have shot George first? He couldn't answer either scenario and whatever other scenario he could come up with, none would have saved the police officers.

Having gathered his thoughts, he telephoned PC Adams, on his private number, just to confirm that he and Sergeant Stone were OK. The conversation was amiable but short with Adams confirming that both he and Stone were alive and well. Before ending the call, Adams assured George that he would call pop over for a chat at round 0730. Not knowing that he would be needed before then.

George decided that a shower might make him feel better, so off he went. He shaved, showered and found some clean clothes. It did make him feel better, it also made him realise how long he had been without a shower and change.

As he went into his bedroom, outside, an engine drew his attention, very similar to the one he'd heard earlier, a distinct sound. This time, he looked out of the window and saw a white Volkswagen van, disappear over the horizon.

"Could it be?" He said to himself. "Why come here? Very dangerous, for him."

He did consider telephoning Adams, or Stone but thought he'd check it out first. They'd be busy enough, having just lost two of their own.

*****

He wandered out into the fresh of the morning, a little apprehensive, at first. After all, the last time he went off on his own, on a mission, he again ended up in hospital. But his desire to find Lilie pushed him on. There was only three options for the driver of the van, after passing George and Lilies house. One was onto Grafton Beck, which was the local route into the new estate. Two was down to the stream and his parents' cottage and three, that was Hope farm house and Elm cottage. "If it is Smith, it's got to be Hope Farm or Elm Cottage." George said out loud. And that's where he headed.

He arrived to a rendition of the dawn chorus. Not even his arrival quietened the unique sound, of the birds, heralding the new day. It occurred to George that he missed the moo of the cows, as they queued at the gate, for their early milking, impatiently waiting not just to rid themselves of the weight of milk that they were carrying but to benefit from the rewards of the special breakfast, which contained molasses. Essential for keeping their sugar levels up and their mood good. An essential treat that, was no more, here at Hope farm. The dairy long gone and both the farm house and Elm cottage, long since having seen any residents. It did seem an empty and eerie place in the mornings now, in comparison with then. He felt sad. for it.

As he ambled and soaked up the nostalgic atmosphere. He looked toward Elm cottage and noticed that the scullery window was open. It was a small, flap type window, that opened directly on to the flat ground on the outside. Inside, it was a full six feet to the floor. As he got closer, he could see that the long grass had been flattened. This made opening the window easier and allowed more light and, of course, fresh air into the scullery. George became nervous, goose bumps covered his body and the hairs on the back of his neck stood on end.

"Hello." he whispered, as if in hope that no-one would answer. But something happened, a shuffle. There was something, or someone in there.

"If someone is in there, bang something, twice."

Bang, two seconds, bang, like a cupboard being shut. Then silence.

He stood up, sharply.

"I'm coming in."

And he raced around to the back door, he found that It had been forced open. He entered into the washroom and looked to his right, the door to the scullery was open. Inching his way towards the door, he repeated over and over.

"It's OK, it's OK."

One more tentative step and he could see all within, quite clearly. The light that he had created from the open door and the light from the open window provided him with the sight he had prayed for. Lilie, his darling Lilie. He careered in, now without fear. Frantically untying Lilies' gag and pulling the pad from her mouth, he then kissed her.

"She pushed him away."

"George, my husband, I love you but we must hurry. Smith told us that he wouldn't be long, just went to get rid of the van."

"George freed Lilie from her binds."

"Go, Lilie, go."

"But George."

"Go Lilie. Go to the workshop, it's nearer and phone the police. Tell them to send Adams and Stone."

"I need to take the children."

"I know, my darling but you can run faster than any of us and without a child to carry, you'll be quicker still. Don't worry, I'll free them, that, I promise. Now, the clock is ticking, go."

"OK, my husband, I love you." And she was gone.

Peter was next. George freed Peters' gag and wiped the saliva from his face with the bandage. He then freed his ankles but when he rose to free his hands, he noticed that Peter was shaking and was wetting himself. Lucy had turned away and was cowering into the corner.

"It's OK, you'll soon be free." Said George. But Peter continued to shake and was staring straight passed George, who turned and was finally faced with Smith, who was stood rigid, arm out straight, with his gun, pointing at George.

"Confident, aren't we Farm boy? None of us are going anywhere."

"Lilies…."

"Gone to get help, yeah, yeah. I saw her running towards your shed but didn't bother about her. By the way, I cut the phone wire at your shed. She'll have to go somewhere else now. More time for us."

"What is the purpose of all this, Smith. You must know that you'll never get away with it. You'll get caught, one day."

"My name is not Smith!. I used my time behind bars, to do some research. Guess what, I found out who my real dad was. His name was Peter Thomsett. He was a lorry driver for some firm over Middleton way. Did something bad, don't know what, then killed himself. So I changed my name, to rid me of that scum family that adopted me. Why am I doing this? Because I can. I have no future, so I intend to do as much damage as I can before leaving this life. No cop is going to kill me, I'll go when I decide and you and the children are coming with me."

"What have I done? What have the children and Lilie done to you? Mary started all this and it was you who got her pregnant."

"Yes, but she chose you. Couldn't have me, so chose you. You and your pretty little wife denied her that and I told her that I would kill you for it. She didn't want me to but, a promise is a promise."

"But the children."

"Ah, the children. See this?" he pointed the gun barrel at his scar. The children are the offspring of the men that did this to me. The ones that prevented me from killing you there and then. I want to make them suffer. As far as Lilie is concerned. That was an accident. I spotted her shopping and I had the idea that it would make you suffer, if I snatched her. I fed her some cock and bull story, about making a family of four. Peter, Wendy, Lucy and…….."

He was stopped by the noise of the sirens, lots of sirens, getting closer and closer, louder and louder. He was loving it, almost dancing to the sound.

"Hear that, farm boy? This is fame, they're coming for me." he cackled, the noise that Lilie hated, he now shared with George.

"Stand up." he demanded, pointing the gun at Georges head.

George obeyed and Smith pressed the barrel dead centre of Georges forehead.

"You're off now, farm boy. Say goodbye."

Before he new it, before he had the chance to pull the trigger, Georges left hand came up at lightening speed, knocking the gun from Smiths hand and harmlessly away.

"Run, Peter, run. Go to the policemen." Shouted George, as Smith made a lunge for him. Smith was too slow. George side stepped the lunge and swung a wide, right handed punch into the left of Smiths jaw, then a left, square into Smiths nose, breaking it into fragments. Smith reeled anti clockwise, steadying himself on the draining board, where he spotted an old, rusty screwdriver. He grabbed it and swung with an outstretched arm, thrusting the screwdriver deep into Georges left side, just below the ribs. George gasped, searching for air, he tried clutching at the screwdriver, possibly the same screwdriver that instigated Cynthias' only childs birth, only to try to end it now. He slumped down. Falling steadily onto the floor, sat up in the corner, no longer a threat. Smith crept closer, for the kill. George looked up and saw Lilie, she had the gun, Smith turned and saw the same but the gun was this time, trained on him, Lilie holding it in both hands, trembling. He made a small move towards her but it was futile, she fired and he fell, the fall and one or two twitches being the last movement his body would ever make.

She dropped the gun and went to George. Shouting.

"Get in here, help me, please, help me."

Two police offices burst in, as Lilie bent over George.

"George, George. I'm here for you George."

"Take it out, my wife, please take it out."

"I can't George, it'll make you bleed."

"It hurts so much."

"I know, my husband but you can do this, You're my hero, my indestructible hero.

"Thank you, Lilie, thank you." He whispered.

"George, please, don't go. George. You're going to be a daddy, George. I'm pregnant."

She took his hand and placed it on her tummy. "Feel that my husband? He's in there, waiting to be your child. Please George, say something."

"I love you, my wife and my child." Was his his last whisper.

She felt his body go limp, his eyes still open but he was silent.

She heard a voice behind her. It was Adams.

"Can I take a look at him Lilie?" he asked. You're right he is a hero, quite a man."

Before Adams could attempt to tend George, the ambulance crew arrived and took over.

While Stone released Lucy and sent her outside, he felt a glow that told him that the Marsdens, the Weavers and the Clarkes were once again going to be a family. Albeit with the exception of Enid Clarke.

As he turned he saw Lilie standing over the ambulance crews. She was crying and praying. Tears flowing down her bruised face, watching George. Wishing, praying, hoping. Too many times had she stood over her badly injured man, who's injuries, on each occasion were as a result of doing the right thing.

"What would life be, without people like these two?" Stone considered to himself, as he wiped away a tear of his own.

He looked at George, who's only movements were those caused by the medical team, doing what they needed to do. Georges eyes, however, were firmly fixed on Smith, who lay in a pool of blood. Gone from this world. Defiance and anger no longer etched on his face. Just a young man, lost in this world. Their eyes were fixed on each other, as if in some stand off, maybe some quiet conversation, of none understanding. Neither of them knowing that they were born within a mere six hours of each other, in the same ward, of the same hospital. Neither knowing that the nurse had made a huge mistake and had given the wrong baby back to Cynthia, after bathing. Not even the nurse knew that she was wrong. After cleaning up the new baby, a sister brought in Cynthias baby, for a change and a bath. For whatever reason there were no tags and, after leaving them in their baskets, for a matter of seconds the nurse turned and became confused. She simply panicked and guessed which was Cynthias baby, convincing herself that she'd made the correct guess. She hadn't. Maybe her life has been full of doubt over that one decision, maybe not but, it was a wrong decision.

So, differences. Did the love and fun filled life that Michael and Cynthia provided, for the son of Peter Thomsett, a rapist, prevent the violent gene from surfacing? And likewise, did the lack of love for George and Cynthias son and a lack of family values reveal a gene that either Michael or Cynthia, or possibly both, unknowingly carried? Was love the difference?

As he was being treated, George could hear the mumblings of the medical team and other hollow sounds as he felt himself being moved and prodded. He couldn't respond. No pain just a numbness, as he watched his male nemisis, whose soul had departed long before his death.

Then, at last, Georges eyes finally closed.

The End

Epilogue

"Good morning Britain. This is Mark Collins on your favourite national morning show. It's 1015 on the 16th of July 2006 and time for our weekly, "What I did on this day in..."

"Today, it's my turn. A little selfish, I know but you'll understand soon enough. On July the 16th 1981, when I was just starting out, I did a gig for a wedding, in a small village near Huddersfield. After a some tragedy and some unwanted twists, which made the bride and groom national heroes, they have come through and today, celebrate their silver wedding anniversary. It's an absolute honour for me to recognise this day for you, Mr George and Mrs Lilie Gilbert. Here's the main song that I played, on that day, on Georges instructions. Great choice George. Here it is. Buddy Holly, When the girl in your arms. Enjoy your day.

Lilie wasn't expecting that, as she was packing a case. It bought back so many happy memories and topped up that love that she still has for "My husband."

"Come on my wife, there's a taxi waiting but he's not blowing his horn...yet". Shouted George. "We're off, we're off, on a holi holiday." he sang.

"Come on you two." He said to his daughter, Amanda, and son, Jason. "Isn't it great, just us four, on a beach in Greece. For a whole 10 days. Yahoo."

"Did you hear that?" Asked Lilie, as they got into the taxi.

"Hear what?"

"On the radio. Mark Collins."

"No. What about him?"

"Never mind, I'll tell you later. Love you, my husband."

"Love you, my wife."

Differences.

A story of love and envy, that asks what makes people so different. Is personality a birthright, or is it instilled through a life of influence?

George. Born to a popular, local couple from a Yorkshire village, he'd led a charmed life and endeared himself to most who met him. Including the love of his life. Lilie, whom he met at a tender age.

However, there was one, who would test that love to the limit.

Printed in Great Britain
by Amazon